CU00726605

INSECT CODE

Inspired by Observation

A novel by

Neil Gregory

To Ronald,

Happy reading.

Neil

CONTENTS

PROLOGUE

Look up the word 'Insect' via the internet and about 65 million results are returned. Such a vast number that it's impossible to know everything about insects. There have been about 1 million insects described from an estimated 7 million currently living.

How many species have come and gone? How many will evolve in the future and fill our world with wonder? There will always be something new for us to find.

Humans evolved long after insects came about, yet we have outpaced them in technology. Humans have learned to study and take the best bits from the world, evolve our own ideas and make things better for ourselves. Better for us isn't always better for them. Look after our world.

INSECT DESCENT

Insect – a multi-segmented arthropod with three pairs of legs, sometimes with wings that are often distinctly patterned

"Ten minutes to drop point, five minutes to running stealthily". The voice came through calm, controlled and without notion of the plans for that night.

The sky was slightly overcast with only a few stars showing through. Navigation would be reasonable on the ground and offer some shelter from any unwanted observers. The craft was quiet, designed to have the minimum impact on the environment, both visually and audibly. 'Make no trace, leave no trace, blend in', was the motto.

It was time to perform the final checks on the equipment. An unusual collection of things, not the usual military style setup. Today there was no armoured jacket, no weaponry, and no massive muscles.

"Waxed jacket – check", a protective and shady coloured jacket from the countryside.

"Camping stove – check. Pans, spork, carbon filter – check". He was getting prepared both mentally and physically. He'd done this preparation many times before, yet felt a little twinge of nervousness. This would give him some edge and alertness.

In this area, the field was covered with dense trees and glades running through it. The water was plentiful, but also dangerous. A filter was needed to cleanse the water from the larger debris that flowed down with the streams. These sorts of activated filters had been around for many years and inspiration had been sought from various baleen filter feeders to trap food, or in this case the opposite: unwanted material.

"Net – check, identification charts – check, pencils – check, plastic tubes – check, lensed stoppers for the tubes - check". These would be critical to this mission. They were all ready and in place.

"Nine minutes", came the flat voice again. Time was coming along swiftly, preparations nearly complete and the target not far below. Although the voice seemed quite ordinary and monotone, it was simply his radio voice. Inside he felt a butterfly or two darting about.

A few minutes of gentle calmness, controlled and relaxed breathing before the next flurry of activity. Perhaps it would be a flutter of activity, but at this speed of descent less graceful than the Butterflies on the forest floor.

"Eight minutes...Seven minutes".

Time was now quickening, a phenomenon of human psychology with impending excitement.

"Six minutes. Stealthy running in one minute".

The chute was in place now, strapped tightly over both shoulders. Bear looked calm. Goggles in place, almost like a compound eye, but without the antennae from the sides of his head. Some great shell case on his back waiting to burst open and spread into an efficient system to enable a good descent. This fall had been practised many times. The simulator tests had worked well, and the field trials had been superb. A new lightweight, strong fibre had been used. This was like silk, but

7

modified to suit the purpose. The wings came out at over three metres wide and weighed only eight hundred grams. The wings were Bat like with hinges to control the surface area and aerodynamic abilities; wider for controlled gliding with fast turns, then tucked in for the fast descents. The Insect Code team had learned a lot from their observations of nature. Would today prove the pinnacle of their achievements?

"Five minutes, stealthy running now active, communication with the coded lights only", came the voice again. Bear wouldn't hear those flat tones again this evening. He hoped he would hear them again though sometime soon.

With what looked like glow worms there was a series of dimly lit lights glowing on the panel near the back door of the craft. They now had five lights lit, each one representing a minute before the descent. They glowed a light green. A calming and natural colour. The back door would open thirty seconds before the final light blinked off. The lights were comforting, reliable and provided an interesting new development in light technology.

The lights were powered by organic battery technology. These become stimulated with a low voltage pulse that sent a chain reaction of enzymes and protein changes to the underlying substrate. A long lasting, efficient and very controllable light source is then created. A simple pulse of electricity stops the lights. These were environmentally friendly, cheap and inspired from nature. That wasn't relevant just now as Bear's mind was focusing on his impending free fall.

One light blinked off. Four minutes to go. It was time to focus on the task ahead, find the base, and map it out. It had been well planned and rehearsed for over a week. Not your normal jump from a plane.

One more light blinked off. Three minutes now and it was all coming together. All the unusual equipment was packed neatly and to hand; the descending kit was beautifully camouflaged and would readily be ignored on the ground by anyone passing by. After six months, there would be no trace of it being degradable and its chemicals would be reused by the local fungi digesting the fibres. "Make no trace; leave no trace, blend in".

*

Earlier that day Bear crossed the dark tarmac at the air field some five hundred kilometres away from the final target site. On the tarmac stood a new air vehicle. It was intriguing. Some things were familiar like the wings, wheels, cockpit, tail, but the colour, its shape and its inspiration was new and unique. The body was sleek looking, but quite rounded, with enough room for a person to stand up inside quite comfortably.

The pilot, Saj, was testing the internal systems to raise and lower the height of the body. Make the body thinner and it flew more efficiently with the cargo squeezed inside or passengers lying down asleep, make the body fatter and there was more room to move about. Adapt to the environment and to what is needed.

The wings could be swept back, which was an old concept. Here though instead of a single sweep back, there were three sets of plates on each side. These could be controlled efficiently forwards and backwards for different flight modes. The wing tips could even be angled up or down according to the tightness of the turns required. Inspiration for the design was from many years of Bat and bird flight research.

Insects, it was found, had limited control of their flying surfaces, but Bats had larger brains, more complex neural networks and needed abilities to outwit their prey in a multitude of different environments.

Bear climbed into the craft and arranged his equipment to be close at hand. There would only be Bear and Saj on this mission.

They got on well together, but it didn't matter tonight. One was the pilot and the other the only passenger.

The control computer was extremely advanced with inter-connecting neural networks. No longer did a computer respond to stimuli from the various sensors and pass information to the pilot. It predicted the flight with incredible detail. Each weather pattern was accounted for and many different modes of flying could be achieved: stealthy, agile or speedily. Some simple controls, changed by the pilot, turned into a complex set of shape changes and propellant changes. The system was superb, but still in development, still evolving!

The back door was brought up, sealed and all was set for the flight. As the door shut both Bear and Saj relaxed a little preparing themselves for the journey ahead.

As the craft taxied along the tarmac the propulsion system warmed. A critical temperature was required for the systems to work efficiently. This was difficult to achieve in the warm humid and rapidly changing environment near the coast. When flying, a constant temperature could readily be maintained in the engines. Biological systems were reliant on a narrow band of temperatures. Tonight, the bacteria on board produced the oily substance burned to generate the thrust. The bacteria were fed on a genetically engineered food stuff with the right balance of high energy components. Later in the flight the fuel would be changed to produce less heat, less power and less traceability in the sky. What fell from the sky as exhausts were simple organic compounds naturally occurring in the air. There would be no trace tonight of the craft.

*

Now only one light remained, glowing positively. This brought Bear into full focus. The door would open shortly and then it would be time to go, to descend and start the mission. The craft had been running on the leaner fuel for the past five minutes.

There was a considerable change in the speed of the craft, now in stealthy mode.

The back door opened. This was the time when the noise increased, wind rushed by on a normal jump from an aircraft; this flight though was calm, the wind speed kept low with the wings at full stretch, at the largest surface area.

Final check and calm. He relaxed his mind and body...jump.

The Coccinelle craft moved away slowly. Its door closed, the body compressed to its thinnest and most efficient shape. The wings became tucked in behind and it accelerated away. There was no trace, no noise and no detection. Saj had done a good job tonight. He showed no emotion and just hoped that the real mission that Bear was doing would work out well.

*

As Bear descended he occupied his mind with names, "Long-tailed Blue, Pasha, Oak Beauty, Glider, Dappled Orange, Studded Purple, Willow Obtulate, Red-Green Flier, Opaque Wing". The classes he had attended were methodical, technical and obscure compared to his military training. The teacher was clear, confident and very knowledgeable. He and his colleagues, had worked for many weeks on the differences between the species. Entomology was a detailed subject, not your normal military activity by any stretch of the imagination.

Butterflies came in all sorts of sizes, colours, patterns and life histories. They relied on many different and often specific food plants. Only a methodical mind would be able to order them all and have excellent recall. Spinning the illusion of knowledge in the subject area was critical. Bear's mission would fail without it, he had been told. That was good enough reason to sit up and concentrate on his learning.

The classroom was small with a few rows of padded seats. At the front was the teacher with the display screens behind him. He had access to various consoles to help him manage his displays. He also had several glass-topped cases on the desk in front of him. In each of these were neatly arranged rows of Butterflies. Some were large and colourful and some small and dull. There was a whole spectrum. These captured anyone's imagination.

Lesson one was about families. Butterflies are categorised by groups of similarities. Grouped by habit, colouration and size. Blues were often small, colourful yet not always blue. It would be very confusing to learn these categories. Gliders had large wings and spent time about the tree tops. Obtulates were a recently discovered group specific to the area in the first mission, a species with more oblong shaped wings. The unusual shape was a quirk from a random step in evolution. No one knew the reason for their unusual wing shape. Now was not the time to question them, just to learn about them, collect some specimens and send them back. Or so he had been told. He had to keep reminding himself that this was the mission: collect Butterflies!

Some days were about cramming names, English names, scientific names and Spanish names. If he was going to be questioned about these Butterflies he had to know all about them. Some days were out in the green houses; large structures of controlled environments, humidity and sunlight. They were all controlled to allow the various plants to grow optimally. Each species of Butterfly had a set of requirements from food plants for its larva to nectar sources, age of leaves and many other factors. Science was catching up with the requirements for each species. More was still to be researched as genetic understanding grew.

The glass houses were evocative places. They were full of interesting and ever-changing plants. From one day to the next a visitor would find different species of Butterflies fluttering about.

The field trips were a highlight of sorts. Something akin to a Victorian outing with gum boots, waxed jackets and a back pack full of pots, tubes, nets, identification books, maps, cameras, pencils and note pads. Modern technology had transformed the field studies with advanced identification from Smart Phones, on-line reference information and Global Position Satellite tracking of insects. The basic skills though still had to be learned. A Butterfly is a delicate insect and a capturing net could cause damage easily to the wings and body.

Make no trace; leave no trace and blend in was the mantra. It seemed apt here.

A gentle swoop of the net and flick, once the Butterfly was in the net was all that was needed to capture it, leaving enough space for it to settle down. The old-style nets were see through and required gentle insertion of the hand with a pot to capture the Butterfly for closer examination. Modern nets could change colouration from white to dark to settle the insect down to make for easier capture. Once in the pot the lid was clicked in place and the pot removed so that the insect could be studied close at hand.

"No harm is to be done", was the gentle reminder from the instructor and none was done. Specimens were taken back to the lab, studied, categorised and then released back to where they came from. Capture technique, study, rename, write details, release. These words kept going through his mind. He had so much to remember. It was a steep learning task.

*

Capture technique, study, rename, write details, release!

A gentle change in the wind brought his senses back as he continued to descend. A gentle descent. There were several clearings below connected by glades. He could see these clearly as changes in colouration of the foliage. Glades he remembered were excellent passages for insects to navigate through from one part of the forest to another. They acted as boundaries between different habitats and areas for courtship display. He was hoping he could land in a glade properly, hide the wings he was wearing and disappear quickly into the forest. There was luck involved in landing when there were no patrols about. Maybe he would be lucky today. Luck though wasn't scientific for him and he had to use all his skill to land carefully, quietly and confidently.

There were several creatures flying about in the night, as would be expected; several Bats chasing Moths, lots of Moths evading predators, finding mates and nectaring. It pleased him to see so many insects. This was a good place to study insects. He noticed the number of small insects was quite large now as he moved on. In this forest, most of the insects were harmless, but could be a little irritating. Many nocturnal insects were attracted to heat and Carbon Dioxide sources as these indicated potential food or places to lay eggs. Mammals were an excellent source of food to be bled and gave out large amounts of Carbon Dioxide. When he was gliding though they wouldn't be a problem. Only when he landed would he need to take care.

The tree tops were getting closer as he glided along silently. There was a general slope up towards the West and down to a valley bottom to the East. There were enough stars visible now to gain an idea of the East and West directions. Good tracking skills would be needed later. These he could rely upon.

Suddenly the wing tip on the left ripped off. He must have caught a tree branch in the darkness, one he'd not been able to see. It put him off kilter and he flailed about. Then another branch. This time the left wing was damaged and not moveable. He felt a little rising panic but quelled it with his exhaustive training. *Stay in control* he reminded himself.

Thump, crack. The wing took a bigger hit and he fell to the ground. He remembered nothing more for a while until he came out of his unconscious state.

BUTTERFLY

Butterfly – a flying insect, often brightly coloured with intricate patterns on their wings, sometimes very camouflaged

The light was starting to increase. Sunrise would be only one hour away. Bear's head felt sore and then he remembered his descent. A lovely gentle descent over the tree tops in the warm air of the evening and then he had crashed. He must have bumped his head enough to knock him out. He quickly patted himself down checking for breakages or damage. There seemed to be little or no physical injuries. He hoped his head would be able to recall all the information he had gained in the previous few weeks. He had learned a lot in the class and in the field.

He took some water crammed with vitamin supplements to give him an early morning boost. It might be difficult to stay focused and energised through the next couple of days if his searches proved unsuccessful. The supplements tasted bitter and added to make him more alert.

What was the plan?

Yes, he thought, *must stay focused.*

He shivered the night away and focused. Task in hand he quickly and efficiently gathered together the wing structures after removing the back pack. The wing struts were made of high grade aluminium and used as the poles for his nets. He kept these for later use. The silken surface between the wings were screwed up tight and he planted them in the undergrowth away from the glade. He sprayed a few drops of liquid onto them. This liquid contained the fungal spores to help start the biodegradation process go quickly. In a few days, they would start to shrivel away and then in a few months leave no trace.

Now was the time to put on his disguise. Not a commonly considered military disguise, but one specifically for this mission. The wax jacket was in place, back pack on, notepad in his right pocket with a few pencils. Pens wouldn't do as they would run in the rain. Left pocket stuffed with glass tubes with plastic stoppers. The tubes were all different sizes. He checked that there were no broken tubes. Shards of glass would easily cut into his skin.

He had a hand lens on a string around his neck. Most importantly he had a net close at hand; a small net with a springy rim to enable it to be folded readily. Then over his back a big net with the poles from the gliding wings.

He looked the part now; the part of an entomologist, a Butterfly collector. Something akin to a Victoria gentleman out hunting for Butterflies, but modernised. He was ready now; set for the mission.

*

There were no Butterflies this early in the morning. They generally needed some sunshine and heat to warm up and their compound eyes were not suited to seeing in the dim light. This would be a good time to make his way towards his target. The target was half a day's hike away. Not too far from the glade where he had landed, and the terrain was reasonable with plenty of interconnecting passage ways. He didn't want to get caught though; swift travel to the objective would suit him.

Now, he thought, *I could practice my skills...find some Butterflies, get the names sorted, make some entries into my notepad. Make no trace; leave no trace and blend in.*

He walked through the glade, keeping to the one side. He would need to act carefully if he was found this close to the objective's base. If he was found, he would be prepared. Being alert to threats and also with a relaxed persona was part of the key to his disguise.

The sun came up over the tall trees and there was dappled light falling onto the glade floor. It created an interesting pattern and captivated his senses stimulating them to look deeper into the foliage. The air was warming nicely, and a few insects started buzzing about; some flies, a few Bees, but no Butterflies at this time. What would be see first? *Perhaps the Obtulate would flap past first,* he thought. No chance of that he pondered.

About ten metres ahead he saw a white Butterfly. It was plain and uninspiring, but the first one today and that was a start. He quickened his pace, he was getting excited, something interesting to observe and find out about. He remembered his techniques to catch it. Gentle swoosh of the hand net, flick it over to seal the top and then dive into the net with an open pot in his hand. He had mastered the technique. It was a natural movement now: swoosh and flick.

'Click'. The Butterfly was in the pot. This is how it is done. He was pleased he had become an expert. Hopefully an expert to those who may dare yet to observe him.

Good, he thought, *I'm in the role now.*

He knew what the Obtulate Butterfly was from all his studies. He could name it, draw it, identify if it was a male or a female and give its life cycle and food plant. The list of things to know was exhaustive and he had an excellent brain to recall the details. Although information about it was sketchy, he was there to find more about its lifestyle and habits.

There was no point in drawing this Butterfly. It was too plain and ordinary. There would be more, many more to come and of greater interest.

The number of insects increased. A Wood-wasp with a huge ovipositor zipped by. The long projection from the end of its last segment wasn't a sting as commonly thought, but a drill to bore into wood and lay eggs there. A harmless insect, yet disguised in its own way to be fearsome and not to be messed with. A grand illusion in its little world.

A few more Butterflies had started flying as the sun rose a little more. The air was becoming warmer and Bear was prepared for the humidity to rise. As the day wore on, the noisy creatures would all be playing out their tunes calling for mates, being happy and the odd one defending its territory. The noise would make for difficulties looking out for patrols.

A large gliding Butterfly was flying part way up a large deciduous tree not far ahead. He decided he'd better attempt to catch this one. Maybe it was the Obtulate, but not likely. His spirits were becoming lifted by the increase in activity. He'd need four poles screwed together and attached to the net to catch this one. It was quite high up the tree. With the pole being so long it would be a little challenging to control the net to catch the Butterfly. It took him a few moments to connect all the components together.

The net made a swoosh noise. This was now a familiar noise from his field training. He caught the Butterfly gently, pulled down the poles to get to the net part. He examined it and this time decided he should draw it. The specimen looked interesting and got his imaginative fired up a little. It wouldn't take long, maybe five minutes to get the outline and some of the shading. He would have to be neat and bring out the salient points of the insect. He'd use thin lines to mark up the drawing with his notes of specific and interesting features. An unusual angle at the wing-tip and spotting along the trailing edge of the hind wing make for a few good notes.

"Good", he said out loud, "this is a keeper".

He was diligent for a while. His mind was focused on the detail. He felt relaxed and content. His view around was calming and natural. His breathing seemed somehow in tune with the forest around and about.

This was progress and he'd moved along the glade network nicely towards the target. He stopped occasionally to study the Butterflies when he felt there was something good to study and draw.

*

Up on the hill side ahead, about three kilometres away, he could see the structure he was after. It had been sunk into the gently sloping hillside and the roof clearly was camouflaged with greenery and foliage. Camouflaged mostly from an aerial view, but from this low-down angle it showed up readily. It had been a challenge for the satellites to get an understanding of the shape and scale of the building as it had been hidden so well. If only they had taken a more side on view it would have been clear.

It was too early to make any keen observations. They would come later.

*

The day wore on and he'd only heard a very distant rumble of an engine. Only a tough four-by-four would have made it along this glade. There must be other tracks, heavily disguised in the forest to limit the visibility from the spy drones above.

There were no patrols. Perhaps there was arrogance from those in the site thinking they were well hidden. Perhaps he was being tracked. He didn't know which and remained focused on the task at hand. He'd deal with whatever came his way later.

Bear spent some time collecting a few more Butterflies, studying them and then letting them go. He had a few drawings in his notebook now, but not the objective of his fake mission; the real mission to find the Obtulate Butterfly.

He had now surveyed the area around the target looking for insects. He settled down about five hundred metres away. It was a good place with a reasonably clear view of the target and slightly elevated above it.

From his viewpoint, he could see the main entrance. Some of the communication dishes on the roof were painted with various shades of green and brown; obviously camouflaged. A few people came and went, and he could see the parking for the four-by-fours around the side.

The mission now was to trace the outline of the building and communicate that back to his own headquarters without raising suspicion. It would work, he was convinced of that. It was such a cunning idea, a leap of intelligence and clever coding that if he was caught he had a bullet proof alibi.

Bear took out his notepad, now with a dozen Butterfly drawings all neatly annotated inside. He started a fresh page and drew a few lines, angular, to scale and small in the middle of the page.

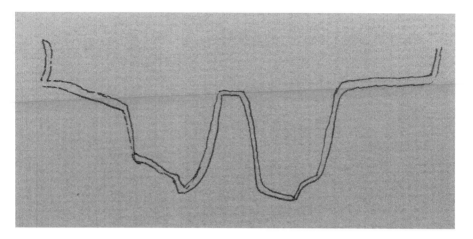

At this point, there was little detail and it had to be sketched quickly, but also accurately. Time was of the essence in case he was caught sketching in full view of the base. The sketch was the outline of the base that he could see just five hundred metres away. His strokes on the page were confident and well-practised. Bear had a keen eye for detail. This drawing felt good.

*

In the classroom, he had struggled a little with the drawing. It wasn't his forte, but the teacher had been good. The class was small and intimate with only Bear and the lady who he had got to know as Martina. She was short, precise in attitude and she liked her music. Just the two of them to teach these drawing skills.

The teacher was a skilled artist and took time to instruct in observations, pencil work and various techniques that would help his skill in the field. A skill practised for many years by true entomologists, but Bear and Martina had only a few weeks. An intense course.

*

Quickly his pencil darted over the page filling in some more detail. He could see clearly from his current vantage point and hoped that he would not be spotted in return. The pots he had used were multi-purpose pots. Not only did they hold the Butterflies, but could be used as magnifying lens to study the Butterflies or start a fire if needed. The glass end to the tube was perfect for this and each had a grid super-imposed to help with measurements and scaling. Now, though, he could use them as long-distance lenses like a monocular; combine a few together and they would be more powerful, but harder to use as they had to be held together. Two pots would work well.

Bear added the detail of the weaponry stations. This was the detail needed for an accurate attack sometime in the future, if an attack was going to be the strategy. That wasn't his role today, just to sketch Butterflies. Any onlooker would recognise the sketch at this stage and he worked fast and efficiently.

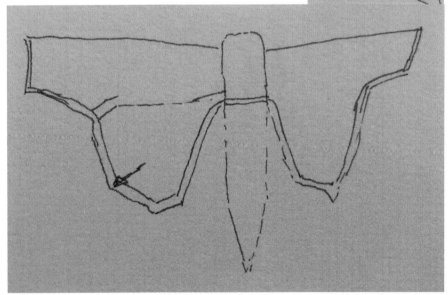

Next, he superimposed the entrances: one straight down the middle was a large entrance way. He'd seen the four-by-fours park up close to here and unload some unknown items. On the left was a smaller entrance, perhaps a personnel entrance. He wasn't sure, but currently it didn't matter. It was the detail of the structure and the exact location that counted from the outside view looking in.

He could now use his field craft knowledge and applied the detail from what he knew to fill out a Butterfly shape. To ensure the secrecy of the drawing he would transform the Butterfly out of the initial shape he was drawing. He needed to do this fast in case he was caught. The disguise in the drawing was imperative to the success of the mission. A strange kind of camouflage.

His mission was to find the Obtulate Butterfly, and this is what he drew now around the site plan.

Detail was important here as there was so little known about this rare and secretive Butterfly. Anything new would be good for the growing body of information about the species. More knowledge for the scientific study. Another piece in the dynamically balanced ecosystems to learn about and study. Insect Code didn't know how much the people at this site would know about Butterflies. The more detail that could be collected then the greater the illusion.

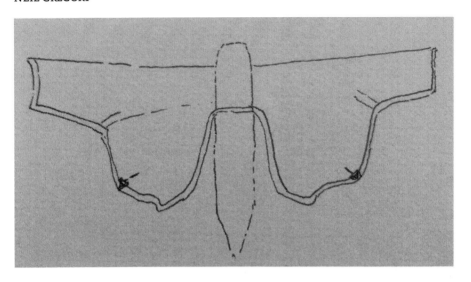

He formed the wings, square at their edges, describing a little of the name of the species. This was an unusual shape for the Butterfly that caused intrigue amongst the scientists. Why was it this shape? Did it fly better? Did it glide further or was it a dead end in evolution? Perhaps his drawing would be helping science and not just to help destroy this base in front of him now? He thought that the mission was to help destroy the place, but that was only his military training talking. He didn't really know the whole picture of his mission. It was right he'd not asked, and he wouldn't be told anything either. There was a trust in any military to believe what you are told.

He started to feel a little more comfortable now, a little more relaxed and a little more pleased that his sketch was panning out well. There was still no sign of him being watched from the base. As he relaxed a little he noticed a few more of the insects about him. A Grasshopper buzzed and hummed and then hopped away. A Ladybird flew in and settled on his arm for a moment then crawled away out of sight. It tickled his arm slightly making him smile.

A Moth flew by him, flapping like a Butterfly in the sunshine; a thermophilic Moth, one liking the sunshine. Many Moths fly in the day time and only in the day time, contrary to common belief. Perhaps there would be some more time to study the Moths later as he moved off site. His mind was wandering a bit and he had to maintain his focus.

There were several critical parts to his sketch. First, he had to be accurate with the placement of the base and the structures within it. Second, he would have to ensure the sketch could be orientated correctly.

He'd already put on the two antennae at the head, but then marked up on the head a single arrow indicating North. He used his magnetic compass to orientate the sketch to what he saw on the land and placed the arrow as accurately as he could. It did look a little odd but he thought he could get away with describing this to anyone with just the one little detail he had seen. Maybe someone inexperienced in the study of Butterflies wouldn't even notice.

The sketch was filling out and looking less like a map and more like a Butterfly. Perhaps Martina would be doing the same thing, perhaps she was behind him sketching the same. Perhaps he would never find out! He might never get out of here alive.

Time for more detail. The eye-spots added to the wings. These were to distract the predators, flash them and they looked like bird's eyes ready to scare away mammals and other creatures that may eat a tasty Butterfly. The wing veins added an extra piece of authenticity.

One last task, to add a scale. It would be obvious if he'd written metres so instead used a millimetre scale and scaled up the drawing using the grid from the bottom of the tubes. A simple operation of scale knowing the distance from his present position to his target position. If he was out with the measurements, then the destruction would not be effective. That's what he reminded himself using his military field training.

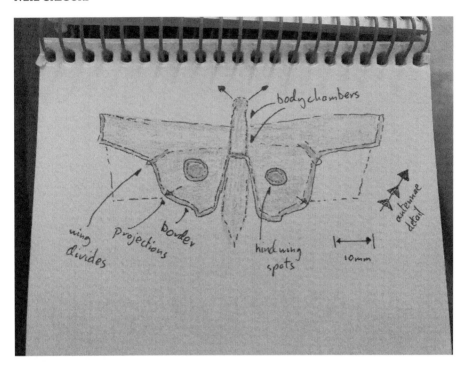

All complete. Now to move away, silently, without suspicion. "Make no trace; leave no trace and blend in".

COCCINELLE

Ladybird – small beetle with a domed back, usually brightly coloured and often spotted. In the family Coccinellidae. The wings are encased in a hard shell

The hanger doors slid open on their runners to reveal the new craft. It was small with a domed back. It clearly resembled a Ladybird, but a black variety with no visible spots. This craft did not have a pointed nose, there were no engines slung under the wings and no tail plane to speak of.

How this craft flew was quite a mystery. It did fly and was intelligent in the way it flew. A Ladybird was a chunky insect and when viewed slowed down many times when flying seemed extremely ungainly and not aerodynamic. Inspiration of design didn't mean exact emulation. The best functions and ways of doing activities were extracted. Perhaps even made better than nature provided.

There was a one-person crew. Today it was a slight man who took the controls. He was light on his feet, agile and alert. As he walked across the tarmac he showed an air of confidence. Although an autonomous craft, the Coccinelle today would be handled by an operator. On test flights having a human brain on hand to problem solve was a great advantage. Computers had developed rapidly recently, and artificial intelligence was appearing in more and more products, but at this stage in developments the risks were high with emerging technology. A human was therefore needed to supervise the electronics and the programming.

The Coccinelle took inspiration from nature in many ways. The pilot was going to explore the features greatly today and push the envelope of flying hard. One obvious feature of the craft that had limited inspiration from nature were the wheels. These were fundamental to movement on the ground and nature had very few examples of freely rotating structures. Some flagella are found in bacteria that have whip like tail that rotate to help propulsion. Humans had out surpassed evolution at times and the wheel was on of human's greatest moments of inspiration.

Humans have been using wheels for at least six thousand five hundred years and had become the basis for a huge amount of human evolution. Wheels were used for making pottery, wheels for moving goods, wheels even to move on the moon. Today though they were set out underneath the craft to help it move the short distance along the taxi-way. Once tucked away neatly in the belly of the craft there would be no sign of craft as it effortlessly streaked across the sky.

The pilot had on a set of ear phones, ironically making him look like the compound eyes of a fly or other insect. *An insect within an insect*, he amused himself with his own humour. The controls were like other planes with a yoke, pedals and power controls. The displays were gently glowing indicating the engine status, air speed and the usual metrics for flying. There was not much room for the electronics, but the new Three-Dimensional chips enabled a cube of processing power to be slotted in below the pilot's seat. Previous banks of chips would have been needed to be laid out in layers taking up much more room. Moore's Law of multiplying power with diminishing size of chips didn't consider these Three-Dimensional innovations.

The domed back on the Coccinelle looked smooth and dark. The pilot came up to the craft and ran his finger gently over part of the skin. The outer layer was not very smooth, but very slightly pitted and ridged. This helped the flow of the air around the shape like a golf ball's dimples. The leading edges of the wings had tubercles like those found in various whales to help the fluid flow over their skin. Any oncoming radar would bounce off these pits randomly and disrupt any signal. Lots of inspiration from nature. His fingers felt these surface features and it gave him a sense of confidence.

A Bat can catch a Moth if the echolocation sounds bounce back strongly enough. If the sounds get absorbed or reflected in many directions, then the Moth has a better chance of evading the predator. That was the principle being used here. Radar signals would simply disperse away. If a signal was received back it would be very weak.

The wings remained in their forwards position. The pilot wiggled the wing tips in the pre-flight checks ready for use later. He could almost feel the wings moving as extensions of his own body.

He moved a slider on the console in front of him with his finger tip. Delicately sliding across the glass like surface. The domed back of the craft began to compress into a more streamlined shape. It had been a significant step in aircraft design to have a body that acted as a wing to provide extra lift rather than the lift only coming from the wings. This change in shape meant there would be the least drag effect when a small payload was being carried. The body could then be expanded to accommodate a larger payload but would be less streamlined. It could be adapted according to the need at hand.

The dome compressed about one metre. Very impressive considering the craft was only two and a half metres tall from its belly to the top of the dome. The pilot was in a recumbent position now and although had restricted visibility forwards, if he could see out of the cockpit now, his view would be superb. The scientists had developed a display system that was very light and relied on small cameras around the craft. The images were displayed on the screens, projected upwards. Moving his head about moved the images so the pilot would have an excellent view all round. He could even see below him, which would usually be hidden from view by the floor. There was no need for windows making for a stronger and lighter structure.

The pilot felt comfortable, relaxed and ready for a challenging yet enjoyable flight.

*

"Coccinelle One to tower, ready for take-off", he spoke gently and quietly into his microphone. The craft was waiting at the end of the runway with engines gently humming. Humming very quietly, almost insect like in its sound, not forced or angry.

"Tower to Coccinelle One, please confirm flight duration," came back the controller's voice with equal calm and controlled tones.

He checked his displays to confirm. "Coccinelle One to tower, forty-five minutes."

A search party would need to go out if he had not returned within the time set out. It would be a stealthy flight test today.

"Tower to Coccinelle One, confirmed forty-five minutes. Free to take off when ready. Over and out."

A jet aircraft would start to roar at this time with a long blue cone of exhaust behind the engines. It was such a contrast with this craft. There was little noise, little wastage of sound and energy. It was a highly efficient craft.

For take-off, the wings were kept in a swept forwards position to maximise the surface area for lift. The craft picked up some speed and surprisingly quickly gained lift and eased itself up off the ground. The wheels quickly tucked away, unlike the ungainly legs of the inspired Ladybird. The craft banked to the left away from the control tower into the evening's red glow of dusk. A romantic image of flying out into the setting sun to lands beyond.

This was a test flight with little romanticism.

*

The pilot had a series of tests to perform. He swept the wings back to gain speed and efficiency when flying. The wing tips flexed a little as he made his turns. Clever engineering required the wing tips to be flexible, stiff yet controllable.

His instrumentation detected the various radar signals that were trying to detect him. He wouldn't know if he was detected until the end of the test flight. The engineer had done a great job installing the special skin for the plane. A shark was sleek with a skin like this one and needed to approach fast and stealthily. He had confidence that it would work successfully.

The next test was a dangerous one. He would be putting the Coccinelle into its slowest speed mode. This would enable greater manoeuvrability, but slow speeds increased the risk of stalling. It would need to be done at some altitude. It was also dark outside, and orientation would be challenging. He would need to rely upon his instrumentation a lot rather than his sense of orientation in space.

He climbed up to three thousand metres. A reasonable height for these manoeuvres, but rather high for its natural counterpart: the Ladybird. It rose swiftly with the wings swept back, fuel on full burn and the dome compressed down. The most efficient flying state for speed.

He levelled out smoothly and started his aerobatics. He pulled back on the power, energy being now used up more slowly than before. The wings were swept into a forwards position for the greatest agility and he raised the dome. The wings moved rapidly forwards and the craft slowed readily.

It took more effort to raise the dome as it increased the drag and took some while for the outer shell to change shape. Too fast and the shell would potentially crack and that would be disastrous, too slow and he would reduce the time in the air needed for the tests. The rams hummed gently, and the dome expanded. The Coccinelle looked like it was enlarging to become more fearsome when facing a predator. A Ladybird uses its warning signals on its elytra rather than being larger than usual. The elytra is the outer casings protecting the wings underneath and the delicate abdomen. The pilot was that delicate inner core, but very protected tonight.

The craft was all set in its slowest flight position. He pulled his yoke hard to the right and forwards. The craft rolled to the one side. It wasn't a violent manoeuvre and the artificial intelligence added smoothing to all changes in direction. The wing tips adjusted gently to increase the turn ability. The craft descended rapidly. He pulled up hard to level out the flight. The G-forces increased enough to push him hard into his seat. Insects must experience some changes in G-force when flying, but nothing of this magnitude. There were no sounds from the craft beyond the rush of wind outside; there were no groans or signs of weakness from the super structure.

He levelled out for a moment and then pulled hard up to flip the craft over whilst gaining height. He then rolled the craft back to right side up. A perfect Immelman, as it was called in the trade.

His instruments had worked well, he was level and still at a safe altitude. He had done these manoeuvres before and prepared his body for each one tensing to hold in his stomach at the right time.

He now entered the stealthiest mode possible. The wings swept back, dome compressed, and various probes and instruments were retracted to the bare minimum. The use of various satellites enabled ground speed, altitude and other measures to be accurately taken. The technology had improved with years of improvements to the satellite technology and the number of satellites orbiting the earth. Every decade the accuracy increased ten-fold, although the general public had only limited access with less detail available. Military technology was always ahead of the game.

The engines were turned down to the bare minimum. Various warning messages and lights came onto his display. The craft would do its hardest to avoid a stall. Self-preservation was a key point to the intelligence in the control programmes.

He then activated a multitude of highly visible signals outside the craft. He let out a burst of powder directly into the engine's exhaust causing a bright and hot ball of fire behind the craft. This was the indication to the ground crew to show them his last known location. The radar would be tracking the ball estimating direction, altitude and speed. A visual detector was also used to detect various frequencies, usually infra-red heat signatures from engine exhausts. Sometimes they picked up meteorites hurtling through the sky. This confused the alert systems causing consternation to the ground crews called from their slumber at short notice. Just another meteorite!

He had to use his cunning now to try and evade the ground crew from estimating his position and lying in wait for him. A game of Bat and Moth; cunning and technology; predator and prey.

He was in silent running, stealthy mode. The scientists had studied insects for a long time absorbing details of their niche in evolution. They had developed the Coccinelle from their studies. Ladybird wings had been the inspiration for the outstretched wings of the craft and its shell. The fuel had come from energy release cycles used by long distance flying insects.

Compound eyes of a House Flay had informed the design of the sensor arrays on the craft. This craft had truly come from study of nature.

Humans though, grasping the ideas from evolution's amazing powers of random genetic changes pushing their way through an ever-changing world, made poor attempts at copying the ideas and turning them into real life working objects. The Coccinelle was advanced, inspired and had amazing leaps forward in technology, but was still nowhere near as clever as all the insects on the ground below him now. Even the tiniest Gnat could find food, feed, reproduce and evade predators all on its own. Humans had brains thousands of times bigger than these tiny creatures and made big cumbersome machines that were noisy, polluting, inefficient, but fast and destructive.

Humans had a lot still to learn. In the cockpit though there was only one person. Sometimes all it takes is one person to make a difference and today he needed to prove he could make a difference.

*

He came in low over the airfield. The control tower could clearly be seen and there was good visibility. His enhanced imaging accurately pinpointed the buildings and the radar stations.

*

The tower had been waiting patiently monitoring all the signal systems. They had easily detected the burst of fire the pilot had created for them to detect him. They'd estimated his flight plan, his altitude and probable approach. They had no idea he was approaching.

The dark shadow passed the tower almost unnoticed. The observer in the tower got a fright and jumped back knocking over

his coffee. Coffee an important part of any night workers reper-
toire. The dark shadow whistled gently past at great speed.

The pilot let out a further burst of powder causing a large glar-
ing explosion behind the craft.

Inside the control tower there was great consternation. It was
an old trick many top guns had performed previously to buzz
the control tower. It was impossible to fire a Top Gun as they
were so important for a flying team. The pilot today would no
doubt be getting a dressing down.

*

He landed safely and taxied back to the hanger. There was only
three minutes of fuel left. Too close a margin for many people's
liking, but this had been a test by an expert.

He parked up and descended the steps that had been brought to
the side of the plane. It was a warm evening full of night sounds.
He strolled out onto the tarmac and across to the ready room
for the debrief. He wouldn't get to know all the details – some of
it was classified. The fewer the number of people who new details the better. There would be less chance of secrets escaping.

As he walked, the Glow Worms pulsed and illuminated small
patches of the dark ground. The females had the biolumines-
cence ability and were pretty much stationary. The light would
be visible from many hundreds of metres away. The males few
in from these distances to find a mate. The Beetles had a great
success with this technique. Switch on the light and a male of
the Beetle species flew in. This though also meant the predators
could find them too. Maybe evolution had its downfalls also.

He felt a similarity between the Coccinelle flying stealthily, in-
visibly, quietly finding targets with the Glow Worm's mating
rituals. He had used a significant number of sensors for his task
tonight. The Beetle though had one task and a limited array of

sensors, which though had been more efficient in time, energy and computational time. Again, nature was still ahead of the game.

*

He opened the door to the offices and through to the debriefing room. In the room awaited the Insect Code commander, members of the team from the control tower and various scientists. He settled down in the comfortable seat and braced himself for the barrage he was about the get.

There was no barrage, no harsh words, no stripping of his wings. He remained settled but confused. Maybe the lesson learnt would be told later. Perhaps it had been predicted he would have his little roguishness trick.

The head of Insect Code, Jacqui, spoke first, "My name is Jacqui Atkins and I'm the Head of Insect Code here. That's Jacqui with a Q, like James Bond."

She felt the need to tell everyone how to spell her name using the James Bond simile every time. Perhaps it made people remember her more or perhaps it gave her a sense of intelligence and cleverness.

"It's good to have everyone together in the room now. OK, so let's go through some of the objectives, team." She was a woman of average height, probably aged forty-five, confident and concise. She continued, "Let's get the flight plan up on the screen".

One of the scientists tapped a few items on his tablet and up popped a Three-Dimensional flight plan. It was overlaid with a second trace, this was his actual flight. Both plan and trace were very similar.

"Very good", said Jacqui. "Good flying tonight Saj."

Saj smiled a little smile. He was still expecting to be told off in some way for his final antic.

"So, we can see here", he continued, "where you left the flight plan with the chaff explosion as we planned for you to do". From that point it looks like we could not trace you. That part is true we couldn't, not until you buzzed the tower". Saj's blood pressure rose a little.

"We've been studying you for some while now Saj, your behaviours, your ideas, creativity and cunning."

"Ohh." Saj replied.

"Yes, here's what we predicted". Another trace came on the screen. It showed his aerobatics and manoeuvres, the things he had done to test the plane. "You didn't give us a flight plan from after the chaff was to be released, but we predicted what you would do with the objectives we set. I think you'll find that what we plotted was very similar to your route".

"Well that's amazing. How did you get all that?" said Saj.

"As I say we've been following the way you think and have been feeding the data through one of our recent Artificial Intelligence programmes. You are quite predictable in your unpredictableness".

That took the little smirk off his face. It wasn't anything to be ashamed of, it just knocked his ego a little.

"You can see at the end the second chaff release, right outside the tower. We predicted that but didn't tell the control tower. I like a little fun too and watched the tower crew when it happened."

Saj was a little confused. How could they say I was unpredictable yet predicted what I did? Maybe he wasn't so unpredictable after all! He then realised that if these guys could know what he was about to do then an enemy could do as well.

"Performance report on the manoeuvres please", he instructed another of the scientists.

Up on the screen popped another display showing various charts and figures. The scientist started, "Well this chart here shows the axial symmetry of the wings going...". She was quickly interrupted.

"Let me be clear here", said Jacqui, "I just want the results not the blether." Her slight Scottish twang came out at times. "Aye, carry on she said", trying to revert to plain English.

"OK, sorry, erm, OK. So, in conclusion yes, the Coccinelle performed well, fine, good in fact."

"Thanks for that", Jacqui quickly retorted, "no issues with the frame or structure then?"

"All seems fine from what we've got so far. In a minute or two we should get the final scan from the body work. My team went at it straight away Saj left the craft." Ping. A small message appeared on the screen. "Here it is." Impeccable timing.

She tapped on the message and it opened. It was full of more data and information. She quickly scanned it all. "All looks pretty much OK", she said slowly. "Just a few cracks on some of the minor seams. We'll see to that. We've the bots ready for the skin repair and will get that done overnight".

"Cracks", Jacqui seemed puzzled. "What cracks? I thought we tested the skin thoroughly."

"We had done", said that scientist, but these manoeuvres were a little more than we thought would happen. It's OK, I'm sure it'll all be OK."

Saj had lost a little interest in the proceedings and had started to look around. He noticed three other people sitting a little distance away. A tall dark stern man, a red headed athletic woman and a young man on his smart phone. He didn't know who these people were.

"Saj, come back to us if you don't mind, you'll meet those people later." Jacqui informed him. "Next then is the radar tracking".

"Easy", said the first scientist, "no trace".

"Acoustic detection?"

"Not bad, we heard a few sounds that could only have been the craft, but we knew what we were looking for and are sure they would not be detected by others."

Evolution didn't work like this. Changes happened and if they worked they survived to the next generation. In scientific study you couldn't afford wastage and there was no inheritance. It had to be right using experiential knowledge.

"OK, what about traces of the fuel exhausts?" he asked.

"Nothing sir." The third scientist came in at that point. "There was no fall out that we could detect. We used the air probes to scan for the frequencies of the fuel in the spectrometers and nothing came back".

"Excellent. It's looking like we are pretty much invisible."

"Except", said the first scientist, "we can't hide in the day time. We're a flying object of large size and could be detected with a simple pair of binoculars."

"OK, I see," Jacqui pondered. "Saj have a think, what can you do to avoid the visible problems?"

"Well", Saj replied straight away, "just flying at night should do it." He smirked.

Bear had been listening. He had known enough about the project to know he would be jumping from the craft and a night time descent would be very dangerous.

"That's unprecedented", called out Bear. "How can we do that? We've not jumped from the plane yet let alone at night."

Jacqui simply held up her hand. "Bear it's OK, we have a plan that will work. We've got a few days to clear that aspect up for you. Don't fret".

Bear wasn't really convinced, but maybe at this time it wasn't the main priority, not at this meeting anyway.

*

Earlier on Bear, Oliver and Martina had witnessed from the control tower the operation. The sun had set and the Coccinelle had taxied from the hanger, taken off and disappeared into the night. They'd been informed about some of the technology in the craft with nature's inspiration for many of its radical designs.

They'd seen the craft disappear from the sensing arrays. They knew it was all part of the concealment but couldn't help thinking something disastrous had happened.

It wasn't until the tower got buzzed that they felt some sort of relief at the craft's return.

The three of them had been brought to the airfield today to get familiar with this new craft as they would need to gain some confidence with it and understand how it all worked. They would need to operate various functions on their own. An intensive training course was set out for them for the next few days.

*

"How did the fuel reserves function", said Jacqui.

Saj spoke, "Excellent. It was all responsive and I had enough fuel left at end for another three minutes of flight".

"You were pushing that a bit fine", said one of the scientists. "you know you need at least ten minutes of fuel for slow speed flight as a reserve".

"I know, I know. You asked me to test out the systems and that's what I did. The noise you guys put in the cockpit to tell me I'd little fuel left gave me something to desire!" he exclaimed. "I'd not be wanting to hear that lot again soon."

"Fine", said Jacqui, "what about the efficiency performance?"

"Pretty good", replied one of the scientists. "We were concerned with the barrel rolls as the fuel sloshes around a little and thought the supply would cut out, but it was all fine. The burn mixture seemed good, enough power for the manoeuvres. Why we can't stick to level and efficient flight I just don't know."

"Hmmm", buzzed back Jacqui. "Not really what we need in this project is tame efficiency. Remember we need to have escape routes if we need it and we'd not escape at tortoise speed would we". Oliver laughed and turned a few heads. It was sarcasm, one of his specialities.

"The bacteria", one scientist continued, "did a great job. The bacteria in the fuel tanks produced a controlled flow of fuel of differing mixtures according to what was needed at the time. It was a finely tuned biological reaction and on a big enough scale to be responsive enough for quick changes in supply rate. The high-energy fuels produced caused a build-up in toxins and was only sustainable for a minute at a time. It was all about balance and replenishment.

It had been an amazing idea to use bacteria for fuel generation. Something akin to the rising of bread or beer fermentation, just a lot more sophisticated and a lot quicker.

*

The team went through a series of other checks. It was all good, a few things needed tweaking, but a very successful mission overall.

"Now Saj let me introduce some people to you". Jacqui said and beckoned the three other team members across.

"This is Oliver, Bear and Martina. You'll get to know them in the next few days. And this is the Saj, your pilot. You've seen what he's capable of today, good and how shall I put it…a bit bad too!" Saj put on a wry smile.

"Head, what me bad? No, you're kidding". He replied sarcastically.

"Yeah really". Oliver joined in with his sarcasm.

"So, tell me about yourselves you three. Shall I call you the three musketeers or the three Stooges?", Saj joked.

*

They had finished the briefing and went over to the rest room. It was a place to chill, relax and regain some energy. It had the usual stuff: TV, video games machine, sofas, drinks bar, but also an array of insect literature and insect posters on the wall. It was an impressive collection of information.

"An Elephant hawkmoth never forgets", he said as he led the team into the room. "love this place, full of useful things and amazing facts. Come on down. What do you want to drink? Nectar perhaps", he joked.

Bear needed a whisky, just the one though. A fine single malt from the Scottish Highlands. An evocative nectar full of power, resonance and memories. A drink for an occasion and this had been a great and inspiring occasion already.

Oliver was a Shandy man. Something of a blend of different tastes, but weak tastes, nothing too extravagant.

"I like a touch of the Russian", Martina blurted out. They all laughed. "A Russian Vodka", she quickly added.

They knew now they would all get on. Harmonising with a drink and a chat.

"So, tell me little about yourselves then?" He asked.

Bear started, "I'm a military man and now flitting about chasing Butterflies!" He was light hearted about this. It had been an interesting career direction change for him but felt this was now his element. An exciting and secretive world.

"I've been in various groups." Bear continued. Trained with the best and the worst. You know what it's like, too many egos. I prefer the small team working with a single objective and using my brain a bit more."

"A brain the size of a Butterfly more like", chortled Oliver. His Shandy was having an effect now.

"This is Martina". He introduced her. It was his personality to mingle and join people up. "She's our jump expert. She's taught me a huge amount about falling. Who would have thought it would be so complicated?"

"It's easy really", said Martina. "Just jump, fly and land. Haven't I told you that already?"

"Well I'm a music lady really. That's my passion. Love the beats, harmonies, complex evolutions, contortions and that sort of thing".

"Yeah I wondered what the hum was", chuckled Oliver.

Saj was listening intently. Maybe she had a lot to give. He knew little about music and wondered why she was here. Maybe he would find out later but remembered that this was a secret organisation and he would only be told what he had to know.

"Me, I like a good ceilidh band. Something exciting to get me on my feet and have a giggle about." Saj stood up and did a little jig. The drink must be having an effect to get him to do this, especially in front of new people. "Nothing like a ceilidh to get people on their feet. Discos are dull, just a load of incoherent noises and uncoordinated youngsters."

"Yeah, I agree." Martina replied.

"I've no idea why you're in this project Martina. I don't see many insects on the dance floor." Said Saj.

"So, you are Oliver. I get the sarcasm thing from you. It's a shield, a defence when you don't know what to say?" Saj said.

"Well, err I suppose. Dunno really". Oliver said back. Teenager speak with little content.

"Just kidding Oliver. I can see you've plenty to give. You must be the techy one?"

"Yeah something like that. Me, I'm all about data, user interface and encryption. It's a cool subject. There's a tonne to learn from our insect partners in this area."

*

The night wore on and they got to know each other. In the morning though, the training would start. The start of some mission these four new friends had no clue about yet.

BIO-INSECT OIL

Oil – made over tens and hundreds of millions of years by the breakdown of sea-based micro-organisms. It is a hydrocarbon and a sought-after fuel source for human activity

Bio-Insect Oil was formed at a time when oil use was decreasing, and environmental sustainability was increasing. The balance of nature had been disrupted too fast by humans for the earth to cope. Too much pollution and too little caring for the earth.

Everything had to be "green", although green meant less damaging rather than ecologically sound. Green Gold was the new Black Gold. This was the spin that Bio-Insect Oil had spun to its investors. It would be a get rich quick scenario using an untapped resource from the world: insects.

"These insects are useless creatures and pests", they had said.

They never once said they would be harming whole ecosystems. How wrong they were and what a disaster they would be creating in the environment.

Bio-Insect Oil was founded by a rogue entomologist and an Oil Tycoon, Henry Collinsdale. The entomologist, Bill Woodly, had been respected and a widely-known personality, slightly quirky, yet knowledgeable. He had known that the world needed protein for humans to survive and that insects may be the food stuff of the future.

Bill also had a deep-rooted interest in geology; what fossilised plants and animals had been found in the various rock strata fascinated him. It stemmed from a childhood interest in dinosaurs. The word dinosaur meant "terrible lizard", but this was a naïve name, one derived from a lack of understanding of nature. People had named the creatures when they were first found, and the first impression is what stuck with them. So had the name dinosaur. Dinosaurs were incredibly diverse, and their relatives lived for millions of years; some two hundred and thirty to sixty-five million years ago. It was unfair and incorrect to give this group a single name. Their bodies had been laid down millions of years ago and had remained in the heat and pressure of the ground for millions of years too.

His studies had led him to find out how oil reserves had been produced and under which layers of rock they would be found. He knew that the modern human world cried out for oil. Early in his career he had a fantastic moment of clarity: we can breed insects and accelerate the process of creating oil with the right enzymes, temperature and pressure control. He knew enough to perform some experiments.

He had been funded by the Henry's investment trust to experiment with various insects. He'd bred Locusts, Termites, Moths, Aphids and various other species. His experiments had produced reasonable results.

The locusts were chunky and fast growing, easy to feed and bred fast too. The world had seen real life instances of a bloom in numbers – something based on fact, not fiction. People didn't like locusts as they caused great devastation to crops and greenery if uncontrolled. Perhaps he could find the mammoth swarms of locusts, capture them and turn them into something useful.

It was not to be. The vast swarms were unpredictable in their emergence and impossible to find with all the equipment that would be necessary. It was labour intensive and fuel intensive which defeated the purpose.

His next leap into the dark was to think about extracting the insects from a vast source, a forest in the tropics perhaps. He'd thought it would be sustainable by sucking out some insects and they would simply breed and rebuild their populations. Just what they did naturally to fill their own niche. He was wrong but didn't know it at the time when he went to his investor.

Work started in earnest trying to find a way to capture wild insects by sucking them from the environment. He would need a site constructed in the wild somewhere with all the equipment made available on site.

It would be a large structure with conical devices to suck in the insects using a strong airflow. A pooter, but on a grand scale. A pooter was a small tube with tube attached through which air is draw and the insects get stuck in the tube. This was something he had used extensively in the field to good effect. He'd thought that this may work on a local level. A suction device could draw in from a few tens of metres away, but not from a whole forest. What could he do to get a large distributed insect population? He would have to think about that one carefully.

*

He had been out at night studying nocturnal insects, mostly Moths using a Moth light. The light was bright and threw out rays of Ultra-violet which attracted the insects into the trap. He was pondering then the life cycle of these beautiful and magnificent creatures when he was drawn to various specimens with large antennae.

He knew these antennae were very important for the males to detect, smell perhaps, the pheromones from the females. There had been studies showing that the males could detect the intoxicating chemicals from quite some distances away. Some of those studies had shown a range of up to five kilometres. Maybe more.

That was it he thought. Send out some pheromones in one general direction and the insects would then travel directly to the source. Once close enough the machine would suck in the insects and they would be captured. Do this on an industrial scale and they would have enough insects for the job. All it took was to bring together several thoughts and ways of doing things to bring about a new and devastating scheme.

*

Extracting the pheromones had been quite a simple task. He'd done it many times before. The trick was to find pheromones that would attract a broad spectrum of insects. Each pheromone usually just attracted one species.

He pondered whether there were predators out there that used this very mechanism to catch prey. A bat chases a Moth using sound, a mouse finds insects by smell and sight and why not a creature that smells exactly like a female of some insect or other? He didn't know of any and lodged that thought for some later use.

He settled on the idea of a blend of chemicals. Use some fancy molecule making device to send out little bursts of pheromone specific to one insect and then another and then another. As the technology developed, more and more pheromones could be pumped out. Maybe he would find the silver bullet of pheromones that would pull in all the insects. That though wasn't likely, so he'd have to work through one species at a time.

That was the theory and he'd been working on it intensively. The money was good and that drove him. It also blinded him to any ethical issues of environmental destruction. Henry had the expertise to pull the wool over the publics eyes on this – it was cheap oil after all and that's what mattered right now. All he had to do was get the technology right and working on a large and sustainable scale.

*

The final design of the building was quite a simple one. There would be two funnels pointing out of the building and they would be moveable horizontally so that they could cover one-hundred-and-eighty-degree view. Also, they could be brought up and down to sweep the area. The suction would be changed to a fan mechanism to help blow the pheromones out into the forest. Any pheromones would be recaptured by a clever air filter with activated carbon sponges. A little recycling was always good. The power source for the plant would be solar power with an array of thin film panels on the roof. A little token to appease the investors. It was Green Gold not Black Gold.

The site was camouflaged heavily. Henry knew it would be the target of intense speculation and prying eyes. Several well-trained guard staff were recruited to ensure the site wasn't disturbed. No snooping allowed.

*

It took approximately six months for the site to be completed and all the machinery to be installed. The jungle site chosen was deep in a secluded valley many days trekking from the nearest habitation. Field trials were finally beginning. The forest was thick with flying creatures and it seemed an ideal time to get the plant all working smoothly. Problems would always need to be ironed out and they would need to learn when would be the best time for collecting the insects and releasing the pheromones.

On site now was the entomologist, two site maintenance crew, a driver for the final product transportation and five guards. They also had a couple of sharp nosed dogs for tracking and security work. Quite a large crew until the site was fully up and running.

"I hate all these bugs", the guards were often heard saying. "We have to be out at all hours and they're everywhere."

"You signed up for this", was the usual retort from Bill.

They complained of Moths in their hair, midges in their ears buzzing or roaches in their bedrooms. It was ironic as they were working for a company dealing with insects and they hated them so much.

*

"Team standby for initiation." The voice came through clearly via the digital sound plates. Long gone were the megaphones and chunky sound systems. Sound was now broadcast into an open space via a simple vibrating plate. Some insects projected their sounds with a similar system to project the sounds in certain directions and with efficient energy use. Always learning from nature.

"Five minutes to pheromone switch on". Came the voice again.

The technician worked efficiently monitoring the various displays in front of him. The pheromones had to be kept at a suitable temperature in a stable environment to ensure they were preserved before being used. The temperature would be elevated up to seventeen degrees centigrade in time for their release into the atmosphere in due course.

"Four minutes, now turn on the heating system." The technician slid a few switches and gently brought up the temperature in the small vials. These were located close to the mouth of the machine. It was an evil mouth of devastation.

There was a gentle hum as the fan started up at the back of the mouth of the machine. The fan would be gently blowing the chemicals into the atmosphere, sending out an evocative and intoxicating aroma to entice the insects into the machine.

"Three minutes...". Not long to go.

"Two minutes. Status update please?"

The technician replied through his head piece "All set to go, temperatures stable and pheromones ready for air distribution".

All the humans had been brought inside and the guard dogs put away in the cages. Any human or animal smells in the air would likely put off various insects from migrating towards the origin of the smell.

"One minute. Get ready."

*

The crew at the jungle machine were all used to insects and wildlife being about. They did not notice the first Moth from Insect Code arrive and settle close by. This Moth was sampling the air, finding out what all the fuss was about. It would take fifty tiny air samples each laden with whatever was hanging in the air. This little robot Moth would store the samples and take them back to Insect Code. A clever disguise with an important purpose. Insect Code fighting against Insect Oil.

*

"OK, go now".

The technician then synchronised a few sliders. This was something Martina would be very used to doing with her music mixing deck. Martina though wasn't here. It was the rogue entomologist not a musician operating.

The fan whirred a little more and the tiny valves opened and closed in sequence. A few million molecules of each pheromone were released in a tiny stream over twenty seconds. Once one set was done, then the next set was released. There were now forty such pheromones. The whole cycle repeated every 15 minutes. Sending out all the pheromones in one go would likely cause confusion in the atmosphere.

The fan pushed the chemicals out into the evening air. The giant funnels were gently moved in an oval sweep taking in much left and right movement and a little up and down movement. They swept across quite quickly to ensure the distribution into the air. Twenty seconds for each pheromone.

The funnels were lined with an extremely non-slip coating. This had been inspired from a Pitcher plant to produce the bio-inspired liquid repellence technology. That was a mouthful to say, so they referred to it as non-slip. An insect would land at the mouth of the Pitcher plant attracted by the sweet smell, loose grip and slide down into the vat of digestive enzymes at its base. Insect Oil had used it here to ensure that no pheromone stuck to the side of the funnel.

It took some sixty minutes to empty all the vials. Four cycles in total. Each monitored in turn and pumped out into the atmosphere. An insect in the area would be drawn to the source. Already some small swarms were being created. It would take some time to collect enough insects at the funnel before they would be sucked in.

After a further fifteen minutes the air was becoming full with frenzied male insects. The Moths flew in first as fast and strong fliers, then many other insects. The saying about Moths to a flame here was apt, but cruelly so.

Whenever there were insects there were predators waiting to munch their way through them. This session was no exception. There were several different bat species flying about and the Geckos had become interested too. These were cleverly put off with various high-pitched sounds carefully chosen to baffle and block the echolocations from the Bats. It seemed to work as the predators came in close and then were quickly frightened away. The least amount of prey taken would mean greatest profit for Insect Oil.

The fans in the funnels were reversed and they started to suck in the air. The insects were drawn in and could not fight the strength of the air current. They were pulled faster and faster towards their prospective, elusive and fake mates.

The machine was a callous device and as the insects got to the end the of the funnel, they were brought through several stages of destruction. The larger insects were quickly dispatched and were passed through several smaller and smaller grinding wheels. The wings were torn off and the bodies pulped into a fine soup of proteins, enzymes and other basic organic molecules.

The liquid oozed into a vat which was gradually filling up. The pulling power of the machine was extraordinary, and the amount of liquid was building rapidly.

Once the vat was full it was quickly swapped for a new one. The full vat was moved automatically to another area in the building. It was positioned in a hot place and aligned underneath a large piston, which came down into the liquid. The force of the piston was massive, and the temperature increased with the pressure. A simple fact of physics acting here.

*

It took a mere five days for the insect juices to be changed into something more like crude oil. The volume had decreased a little once the pressure was released as the liquid changed composition. The liquid was stickier now and looked more like the Black Gold. It was ready for transportation away for sale.

*

On that night, there were enough insects for ten barrels full of insects now turned into Bio-Insect Oil. That was a reasonable haul and a healthy sum of money would be made from that operation. The oil was good quality with limited wastage, a few odd wings and things that got through the process unharmed or left intact. Any unused bits were dumped outside the building. More insects would feed on the remaining bits bringing more into the machine was the theory.

*

Bill gathered together his data and packaged it all up into an email and tapped send on his tablet. The information was sent via the upload link through the satellite dishes on the roof of the building.

He had no idea that his data was being subtly corrupted. He sent his reports regularly. He didn't get a reply usually, but that was OK. He had a job to do and just got on with it. There was no need for feedback currently.

*

There was one Dragonfly that was not captured by the machine. He didn't notice this one flying away after the site was shut down for the night. It was no ordinary Dragonfly and not influenced in the same way as the naturally occurring insects.

*

It was getting late that evening and the work was done. The machine was switched off and as much of the pheromones released had been recaptured and processed from any stray females that had entered the machine. A form of recycling of materials. Green idea, but not done in an environmentally sensitive manner.

The lab could produce a new batch of all the pheromones in seven to eight hours. It was a tricky and time-consuming process, but vital to the work. He would leave the machine going for the rest of the night and do some more capturing in the morning. About two runs could readily be achieved in a whole day. Perhaps he could work on increasing the through put.

He said out loud: "Now for some jungle juice." He laughed out loud at his own ironic joke. He wouldn't get sick of telling that joke for a while.

*

Henry's marketing was on full stretch. He'd done press releases and adverts on various local websites. It was a Green Gold future from a sustainable and biodiverse source. It was spin, just giving what the consumer wanted and not what they didn't need to know.

Oil had been a get rich quick and very rich, very quickly. The nodding donkeys in Texas had been widespread and numerous pumped their way through the day and night. That was money flowing all the time. Their numbers had significantly reduced over recent years as the environmental impact of crude oil extraction and its use had evolved. There was such a greed and perceived need for oil in the modern world. There were vast untapped natural resources and many different types of extraction had been tried over the years. Nodding donkeys were old fashioned and only suitable for near surface oil reservoirs.

Had the Bio-Insect Oil cracked the problem of a sustainable energy supply? Using the sun to grow plants, extract carbon dioxide from the atmosphere that enabled insects to flourish seemed like a clever way forward. It was indeed novel. Time would tell whether the consumers took to it or not. Would they see through the spin to see what was really going on?

RECRUITMENT

Aphid – a small sap-sucking insect, about to reproduce by cloning. One after the other popped out, all the same. There was no evolutionary pressure to make anything different. Aphids seemed to be at the end of their role, their evolution

It was only six months before his Butterfly adventure. Bear dug in deep.

His camouflage was cleverly applied to blend in with a diversity of backgrounds. Technology had yet to catch up on the chameleon's type changes of skin tones. Human technology had used infra-red cameras to detect heat signatures and visual light to detect light patterns. A chameleon changed its emotional status to blend into the background. Humans were not stealthy enough yet.

Bear had to use his guile to outwit technology.

It was not possible to tell what advanced detection systems were being used in the field. The enemy always kept their secrets close at hand. Spying worked to some degree but capturing a device would tell a lot about what clever innovations were being used. Capturing an Enigma machine in 1944 helped crack the Enigma code then, so why not now?

Bear had been taught to evolve his thinking, his ideas and his strategies in the field.

Evolution took many years, decades or centuries. It took a long time. Many generations were required to be passed before changes could be made. Make a new life by bringing together two separate strands of DNA. A new living entity then had to be born, fed energy and the information of life until maturity. In humans that took decades. In aphids that takes days. Still this would be far too long in a field of battle. Different strategies would be needed.

Bear's senses were acute.

He felt the environment. He felt it with his eyes, observing the flow of the wind, the smell of the air and the undulating land. What would be a sensible path for someone tracking him to take. Track the tracker and you've a good idea how it all worked. Empathy for your opponent, stand in their shoes, think their thoughts.

Bear progressed at a pace. His heartrate controlled, ready for fight or flight.

Practice made perfect he had been told. He needed to perform high intensity practice to solidly store the manoeuvres in his subconscious brain. The more he packed away from conscious thought meant could analyse the situation in front of him in an ever-changing world. His mind was focused.

Bear heard a twig snapping.

His reflexes kicked in to hunker down silently and swiftly. Too fast and he would also brush up against something, cause a noise or visual distraction. That would be game over. What was the noise? Where did it come from? Was it real? Was it a threat? He had many thoughts to deal with.

"OK Bear", came the intercom. "That's enough for today."

The game was over. As airline pilots practised in simulators, now foot soldiers could practice in a semi-artificial situation.

He could be monitored and evaluated. He would be taught the errors in his techniques. Quickly his thinking would evolve. It would take hours or minutes to change. No repeated generations were required to draw out the survival of the fittest.

"Right Bear", the disembodied voice called out from the intercom, "time to come in and let's go through today."

It was hard for Bear to then come out of character. He had been in his zone and it always felt odd to simply drop it all in an instant. He breathed a deep lung full of air and took stock. He calmed his mind and brought himself back into the safe environment of the training hanger's debriefing room.

*

"Great stuff Bear".

The instructor had always encouraged his staff in the early stages.

"We're not going to debrief today. We've got an important task for you. That's why we took you out of there early."

Bear had been confused as to why the simulation had been cut short. Usually there would need to be a natural conclusion to the scenario. Today though he had been left hanging. His training though told him that there would be a reason.

"I'd like you to meet Jacqui", he continued.

In walked an assertive lady. She aired confidence, intelligence, but not arrogance. Military men often towered over their subordinates, but it didn't feel like that today.

"Hello Bear", she had a firm hand shake. Bear would not expect otherwise. In his game he didn't shake many hands, it was usually a salute.

"We've a special mission for you. We've been following you for a while". Jacqui spoke quickly. "Come with me and I'll explain the detail."

Bear started, "Maybe the start will be to tell me who you are and what this is about?" He wasn't aggressive in his tone, just inquisitive.

"We'll get to that Bear. It's your skills we are interested in. They might just be what we need. We've been watching you for a few weeks now."

"It's time for the random question of the day", she changed subject quickly.

"Erm, OK, go ahead", he mumbled.

This confused him a little enough to stumble. Maybe not the best impression to give considering what had just been said to him.

"How are you with insects? Bugs and things? We need to know now before we go any further." She stopped suddenly in the corridor and gave him an intense look.

"OK, that's a random one indeed. Well bugs yeah, I suppose. Not given them much thought. I'm not really a wildlife fan much, they just get in the way of my work. Swat them, move them away, you know to clear my path."

"Fine", she replied. "That's what we had wondered".

"So why are you asking? What have insects got to do with my training here? I'm not usually confused, but I'm getting that way today."

"You'll see in due course." She was being mysterious.

"So, do you want to learn something new, do some good and help us out?"

"I'm up for a challenge". Bear brightened up and started to smile a little. Jacqui could see she had got his attention now and dived straight back in.

"Great. We'll see you tomorrow at 06:00 and start this new journey for you. We'll not bug you, but you'll get the bug soon enough."

Bear started to like what this lady was saying. Something intrigued him about this new prospect. What it was all about he didn't know. He would find out soon enough.

BIO-INSECT OIL
MEDIA STATEMENT

Spin – an emphasis on the things you want to tell an audience and minimise the things you want to be hidden. A Peacock male shows enormous and colourful feathers to impress the female Peacocks. This hides the fact that the feathers are unwieldy, take up a huge amount of energy to make and get in the way of everyday living

The Oil Tycoon was ready to face the media. He was a broad-shouldered man with a large belly. A belly fat on the resources of greed and human desire for energy. Like many Americans his capitalist upbringing had serious impacts on the environment.

There was a large crowd of media personnel. They were hungry for information, a good story and a fight if necessary. They were only after juicy gossip. The Paparazzi had a poor reputation and this mob was no different. Amongst the audience were investors, financiers and environmentalists all keen to hear what all the fuss was about with Bio-Insect Oil.

"Ladies, gentleman and press I thank you for all attending this launch today", he started in his loud, confident, and as it had been said many times, arrogant tones.

"The Oil industry has faced many problems in the past one hundred years. It has been a messy business at times, with bad management of extraction and resulting pollution. Today though the world will change a bit more. We are going to show you an amazing new development in the sustainable creation and use of a revolutionary new oil."

The press release had said to be prepared, to be astonished with the new field of technology, sustainable biodiversity and wealth management. All attention seeking world issues. Technology was forever pushing boundaries forwards, but at what expense? Sustainability was extremely difficult to achieve. Biodiversity was always a buzz word and Bio-insect Oil would be creating a buzz by destroying many buzzes. Protect the planet from losing more species. Did this man standing up on the podium care about plants and animals? Wealth was the capitalist greed coming through.

"We have spent many long hours in our labs creating a new oil from an untapped resource. This resource is vast, manageable, sustainable and forms part of the pest problems in the world."

He flicked up the next slide. It showed a vast swarm of locusts. "Here we see a billion locusts swarming and causing devastation across many tens of hectares of arable land, land used to feed you and me. These pests have been uncontrollable until now. We have found the right incentive to deal with them."

Next, he flicked up a slide with a mass of wriggling hairy caterpillars. "This Pine Tree Lappet moth causes devastation in pine forest in temperate areas. It's a huge moth that has caused billions of dollars' worth of damage to a natural resource. What can we do to stop this from happening?"

Up popped another slide. This one showed vast swathes of forest all brown and dead.

"This forest was a thriving place, full of diverse life. You see that destruction? That is all from a single insect called the Deciduous Skeletoniser[1]. That's another moth that munches through the leaves causing vast amounts of destroyed woodland. It's uncontrollable and a serious health problem to our plant."

His tone was serious and strong. His body language was assertive, almost aggressive. He was on a mission and he would succeed.

"So, ladies and gentlemen what can we do to stop these insects from destroying our planet so much?"

The next slide was bright and stark in contrast to those preceding it. It showed a land with trees, insects and animals all thriving.

"Here you see a balanced system. Life is good here without the destructive forces of pests. So how have we created this you ask?" he asked rhetorically. His spin continued.

"We have a new system to extract the pests and turn them into a useful product, a financially secure and rewarding product. A product you'll love as it helps our planet and helps humans survive".

"Let me introduce to you a new solution to the world's problem: Bio-Insect Oil."

He paused for dramatic effect as he flicked on the next slide. It showed a container of oil surrounded by happy smiling people peering at it. A slightly yellow-brown liquid could be seen in the container.

"This", he continued, "is Bio-Insect Oil. We've extracted the pest species from the forest you saw earlier and turned them into this liquid gold, a Green Gold with a sustainable future."

"Our top scientists have made a process to capture the pests and only the pests and turn them into a highly profitable consumable product. It's been independently verified to have extremely refined chemicals and cause forty five percent less pollution from cars that are fuelled from crude oil."

"We are soon to start full scale production. We'll be in your market place very soon. The launch date will be released to the press in two weeks' time."

"I know you'll be impressed. It's a bright and green future for our energy needs." He paused for reflection.

"Any questions?" He asked.

A lot of hands shot up. He pointed to one lady in a smart business suit.

"Yes you", he called out.

"Hello sir, my name is Trudi Lynch from The Independent Financial Trading Association. I would like to ask about your investments. So, you have a team of backers here. What's your return rate and have you published figures?"

"Yes, of course my figures are published. Follow the links on the press release. We are estimating fifty five percent value added to our products. The return therefore will be profit in only three and half years."

"Next", he barked not allowing a further comment or question. It was a rapid return and maybe too rapid.

"Right, you there."

He pointed a man in the middle with an unkempt beard and green tie.

"My name is Frank Goodfellow from Green Saviour Fund. What's your environmental record in the…"?

He was interrupted.

"We've not going to answer those types of questions today. Sit down" was his terse repost.

Frank was astounded by the reply and too shocked to say anything. How rude he thought, what is he hiding?

"Next". He barked again.

He pointed to a tall man with a large tablet computer at hand. "You'd better have a decent question". He chomped.

"Yes sir. I'm Huan from the South American Press and Journal. You've said that this is very profitable, and we are pleased with that. Tell us more about the land impact?"

The Tycoon shifted a little uncomfortably and then chuckled.

"It's easy, there will be no negative impact. This extraction is green, revolutionary and will be extracting only the pests. It's going to benefit the forests no end to make a more sustainable and biodiverse place for use all."

He had fallen into the marketing mode again, spinning the spin and avoiding the question.

He flicked up another slide with some figures and pie charts.

"Here are the projections. You can clearly see the rate of growth."

"It's time to wrap up now", he continued.

The crowd was bursting to ask more questions.

"See the press release for more details. Thank you and good bye."

It had been a short press conference and had intended to get people's interest, get them intrigued by telling them only just enough to get them going. A whirlwind of spin.

The crowd was unsettled and some clamoured for more questions. A deputy came on stage and reiterated that there were no more questions now and that it was time to leave. It felt like a political rally for an unliked politician. There had been many unliked people such as this. Ones that had come in with a strong story full of assertion about doing the right thing and then leaving the audience hanging when they'd not wanted to answer uncomfortable questions. These politicians often got their way through spin and subverting the truth. They left their mark on the world with a scar and they didn't last long on the public stage.

*

The head of Insect Code was at the back of the room. She got up quietly and in an unassuming manner having got all the information she needed for her secret government organisation. No fuss, no attention, just discreet. She wasn't followed this time. If she had been followed she could act as a journalist no problem.

INSECT CODE
MEETING

*Social Insects - any of numerous species of insects that
live in colonies and manifest three characteristics: group
integration, division of labour, and overlap of generations*

The Head of Insect Code had called a meeting, an urgent meeting. It was 06:00 in the morning. What was this Bio-Insect Oil all about? She had been at the meeting the other day and was deeply troubled. Why had the environmental question been avoided and dismissed? Why was the press statement so short? Who was this Tycoon, what was his history?

She would need a suitable team to help her investigate. She had a large team at her disposal. This team would need to work together and integrate their thoughts carefully to find out, investigate and plan. They would need to involve a diverse set of skills dwelling on the experiences of the past with the previous investigations and then formulate concrete plans to move forwards with the investigations. It would need a strong team.

First to arrive was Martina. As usual she was plugged into her headphones. She immediately removed them as she came into the meeting room.

"Hi, how's the beat going?", she asked.

Jacqui was well used to her use of language and smiled a friendly smile.

"Sit down and make yourself at home, the others will be along soon."

Bear arrived shortly after and then Oliver. Also, for the meeting a few scientists arrived, not your typical white coated laboratory types, but clever, intellectual people.

"OK, we are all here now, except Fred Jones. He'll join us on the video conference shortly. He's away on some trip checking out some stuff for us."

"Right team, I've brought you here today to find out more about this company Bio-Insect Oil."

The words always made people think of a sermon, but that was an outdated old-fashioned concept. It was time to move on, evolve.

"You've all seen the press release now. I was there. You may not have seen me at the back of the room. There seemed to be no suspicion about me being there. We'll have to see how this progresses from here. We're deeply concerned about this company, how they think this is environmentally sound and how they are extracting pests from the environment."

"Pests," she continued, "as we know are only a human interpretation of insects causing damage to something that they want for themselves. Pests don't really exist. So, what's he saying about these things?"

She was interrupted by a signal coming in through the display screen built into the wall.

"Hello Fred", she said as the signal connected. The video was clear and the sound crisp. The video conferencing technology was so advanced now with superfast internet connections in virtually all parts of the world.

"Hello Ma'am. I've got some good stuff for you." Fred replied.

"OK Fred, let's hear it."

"Well we've already found the first site. They've constructed a building and a road along to the site. It seems to be of reasonable size."

"How do you know it's Bio-Insect Oil?" said Martina with her inquisitive mind.

"We are pretty sure it is them. We've intercepted several transmissions although we've not been able to fully decrypt them. Jacqui will tell you what lengths we've gone with our artificial intelligence already to decipher it all".

"OK", replied Martina.

Frank continued, "there are a few repeating patterns that are consistent with Bio-Insect Oil as an encrypted bit of text. Patterns seem to be their down fall. We're working on it further as we speak."

"So, if you know where the place is", started Bear, "we can track it, send in drones or something to track it all down and find out exactly what's going on at the place?"

Jacqui replied, "yes we could, but that would be too obvious wouldn't it Fred?"

Fred nodded in agreement.

"What we need to do is more secretive and use our skills to their best effect. We've some ideas already, but we need to discuss as a team where our strengths lie and how to work this through."

"You know that Insect Code is an organisation that finds its inspiration from the insect world to combat important and challenging world problems. At Insect Code we've been going for seven years and have learnt a lot about the insect world that

70

we did not know before. As you know we've even sold a few concepts to Silicon Valley to develop new and creative artificial intelligence solutions. We've more in the pipeline too."

"So far, we've studied Grasshopper signals, Click Beetle noises, Glow Worm and Railroad Worm bio-luminescence and various other insect communications. We've broken into the phero- mone side of things too, which is handy for this issue we have at hand."

"What exactly is the issue we have at hand?", Bear asked.

Fred jumped in here.

"I've seen some of the devastation already with my own eyes. It wasn't easy getting near the site. I got within one kilometre ac- cording to the Global Positioning Satellite location. There was a lot of activity and noise in the area and couldn't risk a closer look. You would have thought there would be a load of insects about, but it seems that the forest is getting destroyed bit by bit by having its life sucked from it. So far, we don't know how this is exactly happening. We need to find some ways to get in closer and find out more."

"It seems that the site is taking more than the pests from the environment. As I got closer to the site there were fewer insects. None of the usual things you would expect to find in such a forest like the range of Butterflies, the noise of various chirping hoppers and Cicadas. I had a strong feeling that there was some- thing wrong with the environment there."

Oliver now joined in, "so we have a strong suspicion that Bio-In- sect Oil had lied to us about taking only pests?"

Jacqui replied, "yes that's right. We believe that Bio-Insect Oil has pulled the wool over many people's eyes."

"More of a carapace than wool", chuckled Oliver.

"Very funny Oliver", smirked Martina.

"There are no reported pest problems in that part of the world." Fred came in. "We're tracking all the pests from the globe now. Nothing within a thousand kilometres of Bio-Insect Oil's site."

Bear had been pondering this and now said "this sound intriguing. I'm in on this. I'd love to get to that place and see what it's all about. Do you know what the security is like?"

"There's maybe three guards and a couple of guard dogs. I think they probably use only limited technology there as it's very remote. I couldn't walk up to the front door as something was going on. Perhaps they were constructing something or other. Our satellites can't pick up much from directly overhead as it's heavily camouflaged and keeps changing its outline. Something like a massive Chameleon." Fred had given his account. Not much to go on, but enough to spur the others into action.

"Bear, we like your enthusiasm. You are good at tracking, right?" Jacqui asked.

"Sure thing. That's me. An expert tracker", grinned Bear.

"Well what about being a Butterfly collector?" Jacqui asked.

"What's that got to do with tracking a large building in the forest!" he exclaimed.

"Let me explain then. We found some old drawings from about one hundred years ago. Here, have a look." She threw across some papers.

On the sheets were some drawings of enemy encampments and above them were drawings of Butterflies.

"Some drawings of Butterflies and things. So what?" Oliver interjected.

"Those drawings were vital in the art of spying during a war.

There was a skilled spy who took the outlines of the building, the enemy emplacements. He then turned them into technical drawings of Butterflies. He was disguised as a Butterfly collector, an entomologist if you like. He was caught, and the enemies never found out what he was doing other than collecting and drawing insects."

"Hey that's very cool", said Martina. "Bear you'd be great at that." She encouraged.

"Yes, I guess I would be. I'm good at tracking and spying and I can draw a bit.", said Bear.

"That's excellent Bear", said Jacqui. "We've got you down to do that. We're making up a training schedule for you to learn all about Butterflies, how they function and what they look like, to get you in the field getting some detailed drawings."

"That does sound cool", he said to Jacqui. "OK, I'll do it. I'm up for that challenge. So, that's my part. What about the others?"

"Can I sky dive into the place? Take some aerial shots and things.", said Martina enthusiastically.

"Yep. We've got you down for that and some signal processing too. You'll find out soon enough I'm sure."

"So, you're saying that I will be a secret sky diver? That sounds very cool. Anything to help out of course." Martina replied returning to some seriousness.

"What else do you want from us?", said Oliver.

"We need some more suggestions and ideas how to get to an enemy place. What do you think we should find out? We don't know at this time the extent of the site, how deep it goes into the ground and what the vulnerable places are."

"The front door is always the weakest place. There's always a place that has to open and close to let people in or let something out.", Bear suggested. "Perhaps we need to find out more about the layout of the place in terms of its weak point, find out when people move about and then maybe when the machine is active?", he continued.

"Yes, I think you are right. It's going to be some guess work as to how long we'd need to be there to find out their daily movements.", Jacqui thought out loud.

"Can't we use some of our bug technology to stake out the place a bit?", suggested Oliver. "I know, I like the idea of see no Weevil, hear no Weevil, speak no Weevil," he chuckled.

"Well yes you're right Oliver. We can use our 'bugs' as you call them to see things and hear things. Not so sure about the speaking bit though."

"Probably for us not to speak about the plans to anyone and not blab if we are caught", said Martina.

"Ha, yes you are right. That works. Nice pun Oliver we'll use that one. I think you are our three wise monkeys!" said Jacqui.

"What bugs do you have at hand chief?", Bear asked.

Jacqui turned to the scientists to get them to chip in a little.

One of them started off: "We've got a Moth chemical detection system, a Dragonfly to detect radio signals, Ants to infiltrate computer servers to cut communication cables, Silkworms to create a new form of fibre that is more elastic than existing silk...erm...let me see."

Another of the scientists chipped in, "Really it's any flying, crawling machine with ability to communicate with a similar creature or with a base. We can pack in many sensors and scanners in miniature."

"We've got the artificial intelligence all worked up on some new three-dimensional chips. An Ant has about two hundred and fifty thousand neurons and a Bee something just short of a million neurons.", said the third scientist.

"That sounds a lot for such tiny creatures?" said Martina.

"That's not much really", the third one said. "You and I have about eighty-six billion neurons and an elephant some two hundred and fifty-seven billion. It's not just the number that counts it's how they're all put together and controlled."

"I know some humans short of a few billion neurons.", joked Oliver.

"The connections aren't just like wires connecting two circuit components you see. They have abilities to be enhanced or weakened, switched on or off in phases or for signals to be re-routed to all areas of the network."

"OK, we get it", said Jacqui. "Maybe save the rest of that for the bar later."

"So, we can go in and gets lots of information from this place, wherever that is, but then what are we going to do with all the detail?" asked Bear.

"We're going to have to wait on that one Bear.", Jacqui replied. "We have a few different plans up our sleeves. We'll tell you as soon as we have a solid plan."

"OK, then, we'll wait", Bear replied.

"Fine, everyone. We've done enough for today. We're going to get straight into the training tomorrow. We've got a flight arranged for you to go off and learn about bugs and we have some of our other machines to help you out. Insect Code wishes you well in this mission. Let's just remember our stance is to find out things before being too gung-ho about making a plan."

They all left the room a little wiser about what was possible and what was expected of them. They didn't know any of the detail though. That would come out in due course.

COCCINELLE TRAINING

Ants – small insects each with a specific role combining with a close-knit team controlled by a single queen

The one crew and three passengers sat patiently in their small seats. Saj went through his series of routine and structured tasks, checking all was set for this first flight. The Coccinelle was small and beautifully designed with a sleek and smooth interior. There were no obvious bulkheads and the engine located behind them seemed remarkably small.

The engine purred as they taxied along. There was a gentle rumble as the wheels rolled across the tarmac. The little lights on the taxi way and along the runway to mark the route glowed strongly. The glow worm inspired lights were very economical and gave out a clear light. A perfect example of humans taking the best ideas from nature for their own good.

As they headed out to the runway the passengers quietly chatted. They had planned this session from an early hour today. They were quite well in tune with each other now as they had been working together for a while. They were a team of individuals each with their own specific skills. Today most of their skills would not be needed, yet some of which would be vitally required.

Their plan was to freefall from three thousand metres, work together and fly across the landscape to a specific landing point some five kilometres in a horizontal position away from the drop zone. They would need to use the wings in their suits to best advantage and control their descent carefully.

They would jump from the craft in quick succession, so they could monitor each other's flight and assist if required. All part of the team work. Not that descending at up to three hundred kilometres per hour would give much opportunity to help each other. The suits they wore were very streamlined and three hundred kilometres per hour would readily be possible at a steep stoop. When in a controlled descent with the wings spread wide they would fly at approximately two hundred kilometres per hour. This was still rapid, and the landing would be very challenging to ensure a safe touchdown. There was no point in wastage of a team member in such a small team.

The Coccinelle climbed up through the layers of thin mist. It was a relatively early flight following their very early pre-flight meeting. The craft hummed sweetly as it climbed. There was no great roaring that the jet engine planes produced or the whine from the propeller planes. The sound was quiet calming and made for a more pleasant flight. Pleasant only in sound and not the task ahead. Despite its low thrust the craft flew well and accelerated quickly. It was all down to its superbly streamlined surface and shape as well as its light airframe. There was little waste in the highly efficient and technologically advanced design.

It didn't take too long to get to the drop height and only a few minutes to traverse to the drop zone. The craft was quiet yet fast and critically invisible to watching sensors.

*

Oliver jumped first, followed by Martina then Bear.

They'd followed the signals from the pilot. The glowing lights at the door were their means of communication to reduce any chance of transmissions being intercepted. Radio signals were not secure as they could be received by anyone outside the craft. The Coccinelle had been slowed to a minimum ensuring least disruption in the air flow as they jumped. The dome of the craft had been raised for them to manoeuvre around inside for them to get into the jump position. Bear being quite tall found it the hardest to move about, but he was supple enough for this task and eased about deftly.

Oliver had always had a little roguish twist to his personality and was to be watched carefully for this trip. Each had been told in secret to watch out for each other, "Have some suspicion", they'd been told. "You never know who you're dealing with. Even your friends can turn their backs on you at some point."

There was a little air of suspicion, but their training meant they covered it well. It meant they'd triple checked their own flight equipment rather than rely upon the others. It was all part of the survival skills needed as individuals. Work as a team and be individuals at the same time.

Martina and Bear had been told to watch Oliver as he may try some trickery in the air. Perhaps he'd do some twists or turns that weren't part of the plan. If he did some moves to show off it might compromise the mission and the others would need to find a way to deal with him appropriately. Their suspicions though were unfounded this time.

*

The flight down was uneventful. They glided in what seemed a smooth and effortless way. They had fallen from the Coccinelle in close succession to each other. Although theoretically they would be descending at the same rate as each other, Bear was slower due to increased wind resistance. He was bigger compared to the other two. Martina and Oliver quickly came up to

Bear and pulled back a little to try and maintain a small group together.

They joined up like a mini-network of Ants building a structure to bridge a gap. This lasted only a few seconds as they fell to the earth rapidly and needed to prepare for landing.

Oliver and Martina broke away and spiralled ahead. It would not be safe for all three to land together. If they had a little room between them there would be some increased margin for error. Too far apart would increase the likelihood that they would be spotted.

Martina spread her wings first. This now meant she could control her speed, direction and could cover some horizontal distance to get over to the landing site.

Oliver quickly flicked a switch on his suit. He could not afford to come out of position for long when descending. His arms and legs were needed to control the flight carefully. An array of little lights illuminated his suit. As he streaked across the sky he made various patterns with his lights. He was skilled in the art of sky diving and felt the need to play about a bit, forgetting a little of his task.

It was very distracting for the others. Bear was almost blinded off course. His eyes adjusted to the darkness and now these alien distractions were unwelcome.

*

They flew across to their landing site. In the training this site was well suited to what they needed. It was a strip of level land wide enough for several skydivers to stretch out their wings comfortably. It wasn't very long, but long enough for the task at hand. Long enough if they made the landing correctly.

They each flew in and pulled up at the right moment. It was a carefully planned manoeuvre to enable a soft landing. It took much skill and strength to slow from the rapid flight to a standstill. Birds had been doing this for millions of years and insects for much longer than that. Those creatures though had evolved to be adept and fit for the challenge. These humans though used their brain power to outwit nature and perform the trick using technology.

They all landed safely. Martina first, following by Oliver and then momentarily later by Bear.

*

Once on the ground they communicated to their main base and were air lifted back. The technology hadn't worked out how to take off yet. It probably never would as the energy requirements for that would be enormous to lift a human, many times denser than an equivalent bird.

In the debriefing office, they all sat and waited for the trainer to come in. The Coccinelle had come back to the base quickly, but the pilot, Saj, had to ensure the craft was safely stowed away from prying eyes and that it was still in good condition. It was good practice to preen once landed. All birds did this and many insects too.

"So, Oliver you lit up the sky?" quizzed Saj. "You're going to get us fired from this mission if you continue your stunts."

"Just a bit of fun skip." He laughed back.

"Did you like the lights? Think I'll get them marketed for a little profit. I'm going to call them Sky Lights." He amused himself.

"No, not Sky Lights Oliver, stupid lights." Bear shot a look at Oliver. "You nearly put me off course you idiot."

"Look we're here for a secret mission. Stop drawing attention to yourself Oliver or you'll be out. You nearly cost a life today." Saj sharply said.

"Look, it's easy doing this jumping from a plane thing." Oliver started. "It's easy, just having some fun like a Firefly."

"You'll be out with a Firefly in your ear next time." Saj replied.

"We need to get this done guys". Saj changed direction and brought their attention back to the debriefing.

"You guys did well today, despite the mischief. The Coccinelle coped well with a sudden unloading from that height. We weren't sure it would cope properly with that rapid reduction in weight."

"Now you tell us", Martina retorted.

"We can't tell you all our secrets now can we", said Saj.

"The flight suits seemed OK. You three all fine with those?"

They all nodded in agreement.

"I would like my wings to be blue though not black." Martina piped up. "My favourite Grasshopper has blue flashes.

"No, sorry Martina, these need to be somewhat camouflaged for jumping behind restricted lines.

"Yeah, sorry, was in my world then when I train others", she replied.

"Was the landing OK?"

Bear started, "Yes, I think it was fine. How are we going to know that there's a suitable landing place where we are going? I take it that it will be in a forest?"

"Well, err, yes good point. That's not my concern really. I just need to push you out of the Coccinelle. The rest of the things are your concern."

"I think we'll be in some sort of wooded area", said Martina, "somewhere with various glades, and meadows. Live on the edge a bit, I'm sure it will be fine."

How Martina knew it would be fine was unknown to the others, but having a positive attitude was a good thing. Say it enough times and she would start to be believed it would be true.

"Right, does anyone else have any questions?" Saj asked.

No one did.

"OK, so I'll file a report that you guys worked well together. There's a good team with you three despite the differences you all have. What we're going to get up to is going to be good."

"What are going to be getting up to then? Do you know more than us?" Oliver asked.

"I don't know anything yet. All I've been told is to get you lot ready for a mission somewhere and make sure that the Coccinelle works well for us."

"Yeah, I guess you are right. They're not going to tell us anything until it's too late". Said Oliver.

"We'll convene here later for some more drills and Oliver I'll take those lights of yours. You'll end up as Ant food if you distract your team like that again!"

ESCAPE

Escape – a form of defence to save an insect from being eaten.
Sometimes a poisonous residue is left behind to fool the predator

He moved away from the site feeling pleased and a little relieved. It would not be sensible to transmit the message back to his headquarters with the detailed sketches. He was so close to the target base and would readily be tracked. He took a semi-hidden route away from the base in the undergrowth. This would reduce his chance of being seen here. Bear's plan now was to escape and get back to safety.

He found a stream to cross and decided it would be good to walk down the stream. This flowed to the bottom of the valley. The stream would help disguise his scent in case a dog was set out to track him. He studied the bank of the stream. It was muddy and teamed with brightly coloured Butterflies: yellows, oranges and blues all dancing about. Now was not the time to stop and study them, but the thought that flashed through his mind; what were they doing? They were likely to be mud puddling, getting minerals from the wet edges of the stream. "Continue to be vigilant and stay focused". He couldn't afford to stop being an entomologist although he wanted to get out of there as quickly as he could.

The stream meandered along and didn't gain much water or speed. There hadn't been much rain recently, but enough humidity in the air ensured continued dampness, enough to create a stream. The stream bed was rocky and hard to traverse. In his combat gear, he would have managed much better with sturdier boots, more flexible clothing and lighter in weight.

*

Bear's background was in single person operations often deep in the field. His field craft skills were top notch. He'd been recruited to this job by a group of agents. His recruitment into Insect Code though was unknown to him. It was a secret task force and his training and knowledge was studied carefully by the head hunters. They had shadowed various operations he had been on and they had been impressed. Sometimes the spy needs to be spied upon.

It had been only a year ago that he'd been chosen. He was taken aside by the senior officer and given orders to attend a specific location, designated by a latitude and longitude. He was told that the outcome of the journey would be paramount to his future. He wasn't given a choice, but he knew, he just knew, that this was something different, something special and important. Now he was deep in a jungle using his skills.

*

The challenge was great. He had been given no resources other than the military clothing he wore. This clothing was disguised to look like the entomologist. A clever set of clothing to help him in the field. His escape relied upon his wit, experience and knowledge. He had to get approximately five kilometres away from the site before he could transmit any information. Insect Code did not know if Bio-Insect Oil had surveillance in place. There may be camera traps, or technology to track signals. They didn't know and five kilometres away seemed a reasonable distance.

Bear continued down the stream. It gradually increased in size, broadening and getting a little faster. The stream gathered a little pace as the slope became steeper. He would have preferred to walk up a stream to get to higher ground, but this way he could cover a little more ground as quickly as possible with his tracks being covered.

The trees were tall in this area and the ground flora looked diverse. There were many colourful flowers with many different types of flower head. Some had large open flowers and were frequented by generalist insects such as bees. Some of the flowers were more specialised and these attracted more specialised insects..

His mind wandered away to think about the Morgan's Sphinx Moth. This was a stunning hawkmoth predicted by Darwin himself. A sample orchid had been sent to Darwin. The flower had an extraordinary length from the open end of the flower to the nectar source. Only an insect with a tremendously long proboscis would be able to sup the nectar. The moth was then found some time later. This was evolution in action; a brilliant and sometimes crazy process creating a vast range of life. Perhaps he could observe some fascinating evolution here?

He wouldn't see one of those Moths in this part of the world, but his eyes kept following the insects as they buzzed about. There were indeed a few day-flying Moths supping nectar. They were mostly medium sized and nothing as extravagant as the Morgan's Sphinx Moth. Maybe someday he would see one or something similar. Perhaps his next mission would take him to Madagascar.

'Snap'.

His attention was immediately was taken by a noise in the undergrowth. He snapped back into escape mode being alert and careful. What had the noise been? He was not sure. It was not far away. He had got distracted by his thoughts of insects when he should have been focusing on the task at hand.

He then remembered that he should remain in disguise. He had his Butterfly net tucked into his belt and swiftly brought this out. It was time to be an entomologist again. He swished the net about a bit in a confident manner as he continued his journey.

A little time passed, and he relaxed a bit although kept his guard. His senses were heightened and alert.

The flora changed a little as the stream got increasingly rapid. There was more mist in the air up ahead. It must the sign of a waterfall or cascade. In a few minutes, he would find out. The flora consisted of more damp-loving plants, ferns and mosses rather than the bright flowers loved by the insects.

He could see that the vista opened up to a grand view. At head height there was a view of the tree tops ahead. There was certainly a waterfall not far away. From the right, there was a track coming down to the water. It looked as if there was a ford here as the stream was becoming shallower. There were fresh tracks on the right. They looked like tracks from a four-by-four vehicle. Perhaps a recent movement from the site he had left behind?

His thoughts now were how to navigate down the waterfall. Perhaps he would see some rocks to climb down, perhaps a path would be obvious. He didn't want to have to climb down the slippery slope. There would be increased risk now if he got wet as anyone would be asking why he was wet when he was looking for Butterflies.

He was concentrating on the track and the waterfall. From the left a sharp voice called out: wait there. Don't move".

Immediately he switched from entomologist to military man and his thought processes changed. What could he do? He was exposed being in the middle of this stream. The voice came from the bank side amongst the undergrowth.

"What are you doing here?" The voice called out. "My dog here would surely love to track you if you run."

"I'm...I'm studying", his voice faltered a little before he gained control, "...studying Butterflies." He kept his focus and brought himself back into his entomological role.

"I'm looking for Obtulate Butterflies. Since you're here have you seen any?" he started to reach around to get his notebook to show the pictures.

"Just stay there." The voice spoke into his radio. "We've found someone along the stream where it is crossed by the track. He says he's looking for some Butterfly or other."

The radio voice came back, "I see him now on the surveillance at the track. Bring him in. We don't have Butterfly collectors in this part of the world. The Land Rover is coming down now to bring him back here".

"Stay where you are", the voice called to Bear. "We're bringing you in. The chief doesn't believe your story. It better be true or you're going to regret being here today." His voice was terse.

Bear knew that this person was serious, and his plan was about to be foiled. He must remember to stay in character, stay as an enthusiastic collector.

He remembered a pertinent motto: "To breathe was normal, to breathe deeply took control. Take control". He must stay in control.

BEAR'S CAPTURE

Web – a spider produces a strong web to ensnare a victim. Some insects also produce silk for protection or like a rope to help them escape

It was now time to spin a web of deceit. The Land Rover came quickly and nosily, crashing along the track. Someone was in a hurry. He was bundled into the back of the vehicle. Inside there were two others and a further dog. The dog was not a friendly one at that. He knew that these were all the guards and the site was now not protected by them. Perhaps their job was so dull that anything of excitement was a distraction for them. Maybe he could use this to work his way out safely.

When they had bundled him into the vehicle they had taken his satchel. It contained his drawings, tubs, net and other assorted entomological equipment. He had complained about it being taken. It was all genuine equipment for field work. He was satisfied that he had completed his drawings and that they in turn were as disguised as his current character intended him to be. He must not let his deceit fail for his own sake and the sake of Insect Code.

"Why are you here?" enquired the other guard in the back seat. "What are you up to?"

"I've told your friendly mate here that I'm studying these Butterflies. You see there are these special..."

"Rubbish." Replied the guard. "No one studies Butterflies. They are just pests."

"Shut it" said the driver to the guard in the back. "Keep your mouth shut. You're always gobbing off, now shut it".

Bear knew more than the guards thought he knew. Bear knew what this site was all about, even if these thugs here knew nothing about wildlife, ecosystems or anything beyond their jobs or even the end of their own noses.

The rest of the journey was in silence apart from the constant crunching of rocks under the tyres and the creaking from the frame of the vehicle. It was a robust and rugged vehicle suited for this terrain, but the driver wasn't respecting the vehicle much and just kept crashing along. It wasn't designed for comfort either. This vehicle wasn't designed for transporting children to school in their cocoons. It was a working vehicle.

*

He was taken into the site through the main door at the front, next to the funnels. This was going to be a boon for him. He was getting inside the site. The weakest part of a building was the door and it had been flung wide open for him to enter. These guards weren't clever at all.

He was taken past the machine inside and his mind was racing to capture as much information about it as he could in a few seconds. He may not get to see this again and this was his chance. What an amazing stroke of luck this had turned out to be. All he had to do now was to be released unharmed, even with a flea in his ear.

He remembered the Large Blue Butterfly had an amazing relationship with a specific red Ant species. The caterpillars were taken by the Ants and brought down into the Ant nest. There they are protected by the Ants and not eaten as many other caterpillars would be. The caterpillar then pupates whilst continuing to be protected and cleaned by the Ants. Then, when ready the adult butterfly would emerge safely and find its way out and fly away. Would he be the Large Blue Butterfly today and emerge as an informed insect from Insect Code?

He was taken to a room with various computers lining the wall. Each was a modern device, slim line, powerful and with gesture recognition. He knew all that as the person sitting inside had used various swipes to lock the devices as he came in. Observation was the key.

The man turned around. "Sit down now", he commanded.

Bear was forced to sit in the corner. At least they had some sense not to sit him near the door. Maybe though that was by chance rather than design. Maybe they'd not planned to interrogate anyone.

Bear was looked at for a while.

"You are an interesting person", said this man.

"What are you doing here? Now don't be facetious. I can see you are dressed like a Butterfly collector, but that's thinly veiled."

Bear wondered who this guy was. He had an idea, but he felt in control and waited some while to get the clues to reinforce his idea. If it was who he thought it was, then negotiation and interviews probably would be his thing. Bear had a lot of experience in this field, he would be fine. That's what he convinced himself.

"I'm waiting", he impatiently commanded.

"I'm here studying the Obtulate Butterflies", Bear started confidently. "I've some sketches to show you in my book, but your guys took it away. Nice guys, but they don't know anything about Lepidoptera. What are you doing here and what do you want?". Bear felt he should be asserting the questions.

"I'm not here to answer your questions Bear." Bear was a little taken a back that the guy knew his name. Had he let it slip in the conversation in the Land Rover? He didn't think so.

He called across to one of the guards. "Bring the bag here let's see what you've got".

The guard brought the bag and tipped it upside down on the table. "Just a load of stuff, nothing dangerous here sir." That's just what Bear needed him to say.

He sifted through the things.

"So, you know my name. What's yours?"

Bear was trying to take the higher ground. Know your enemy, break down the communication and start to open the door to the way out.

Bear was causal and in control. He was trying very hard not to ask like a scared rabbit in the headlights here. His senses were high though, taking everything in. He had a powerful memory for detail and was storing it all; the location of all the equipment, the security features. He was feeling elated that he had been brought into the enemy establishment. The weakest point was the front door and he had just been walked right through it.

"I said no questions," was the terse reply.

"OK Bill no questions."

"What!" the man replied almost losing focus. "How do you know that?" Any skilled interrogator wouldn't open up to let his name come into the conversation.

"I told you", Bear replied, "I'm here studying Butterflies and detail is what I like to look at. Someone had written Bill in your shirt name tag that was sticking out when I came in. I couldn't help but read it. Was it your mummy that wrote that for you?"

"Shut it Bear."

Bill was getting annoyed now. Maybe Bear would need to change the direction and calm things down a bit now.

"Do you want me to tell you what all those things are that you've ungraciously tipped from my bag?" Bear calmly asked.

"I know what these things are, don't patronise me."

Bear was sure now who this man was. He was the lead entomologist in the organisation. Most people wouldn't know what the collecting tubes would be for. Along with these, the reference books and all the other bits all together made a field study kit. This was a boon for him. He had to think carefully what to ask next.

"It's an interesting machine you have here. Do you collect Butterflies too?" Bear thought a cheeky approach would be a good one. "Here pass my book and I'll show you what I've found."

"No, no, you stay there Bear." Bill started to flick through the sketch book. It was indeed a sketch book filled with Butterflies. He knew what he was seeing and read through a little text to confirm.

Bear was slightly sweating now. One little bead appeared on his forehead. Bill though wasn't wise enough to study details in people. He was too distracted by the whole situation not knowing what to do next. If he'd watched Bear closely he would have seen the stress on his face a little.

"So, some Butterflies here." he pondered out loud. "Nothing here, just some poor sketches. These aren't right", he said when he stopped and looked at one. "That's not how Butterflies look."

"I'm here to look at new detail." Bear was trying to go along with this now. "Those Obtulates are fascinating, there seems to be a lot of local variation in this species. There's a load of evolution in action in this place. It's fascinating."

"Evolution!" snarled one of the guards. "That's all we hear. Evolution this, evolution that. There's no such thing. Stuff was just created! What shall we do with this guy Bill?"

The guard was so wrong. There was no evidence in the world that things were created. This was an uneducated naïve viewpoint made centuries ago. That concept had been thrown out many moons past.

"Come on you", Bill snapped at the guard. "You're here to protect this place not to let spill your old-fashioned views."

"Protecting what?" Bear asked causally.

"Never you mind!" Bill was getting distracted by it all and his temper was rising.

Bear knew that Bill couldn't concentrate on managing the guards, the interview, looking at the items and all that at the same time. This might be a good tactic to break things up.

"So, you don't believe in evolution then?" Bear asked the guard.

"Naw, it's just some cranky scientist talking science-y nonsense."

"Ah, I see. So, you're not a scientist too?" Said Bear

"A scientist, you're kidding. You're not going to find me in a white coat staring down a microscope looking at bugs all day. Hate these things me. And all that goo from here is disgusting."

Bill was incensed. This guard was letting out details about this place giving away the secrets. Why had they hired these buffoons?

"Right! One more thing from you and you're going in the machine too". Bill shouted at him.

"What's the machine for?" asked Bear trying to find a way in for an admission. "Is it a mincing machine or something?" Bear laughed.

Bill went a little red.

Bill continued to search through the contents of Bill's bag.

"That's a brick that phone." Bill chortled. "You really are an old-fashioned man Bear. This thing is from the archive!"

Bill just dismissed the phone. Bear was pleased with that. The phone was heavily disguised to look like something useless. If Bill had opened the case he wouldn't find the clunky electronics from the past, but an amazing array of three dimensional chips, recording devices, neural networks and communications technology. The trick had worked. Insect Code had done a good job.

The sketchbook was put on the table. Bear twigged how Bill had got his name. He'd written it on the cover of the book. Maybe Bill didn't lack observation skills. "Remain vigilant Bear", he reminded himself.

This wasn't a real interview; it was very poor.

"OK, it's time I went now. I've got to get back to write up my notes about these Obtulates." Bear said.

Bill didn't say anything. He was thinking now. Racking his brain. Was this guy genuine or was he hiding something? He didn't have the analytical human skills to find out. Bill used computers not people skills. He could talk about the variations in venation patterns in these Butterflies, or the hydro-carbon contents of the insects, or many other technical things, but communication and negotiation skills were not his thing.

"I've not got time for you Bear. Take him away, as far as you can."

This was amazing, there seemed to be nothing that Bill was asking or finding out that made for any conclusion that Bear was nothing other than a Butterfly collector. How wrong he was.

*

Bear was manhandled back to the Land Rover by the guards. He had got his bag back. The phone was intact, and his sketchbook had been left un-defaced. He kept mulling over the site. The details of where the items were located were now firmly stored in his head.

He was taken roughly along the track again past the point where he was picked up previously. The track kept going through the amazing landscape. There was still limited insect life, but Bear could see areas worthy of study. There wouldn't be time now to find out more and no opportunity to stay and study them. He had found out enough already for the mission.

The Land Rover was creaking more now as the track got rougher. The driver seemed to either care little about being careful or was in a hurry for something.

Bear knew that there would be communication outside of the site following his useless 'interview'. Maybe Insect Code would be intercepting the data and finding out what had been said.

The Land Rover came to a holt quickly skidding in the mud. Bear was pushed out. "Thanks for the ride guys. See you soon." Bear smiled politely.

"Get lost!" One of the guards said. "It won't be so friendly next time if we find you here again."

The Land Rover skidded away. The guards must have thought he wouldn't survive in this wild place so had just dumped him at the side of the track. They didn't know of Bear's former life and survival skills. This would now be a breeze to escape from and get back to Insect Code with all the information he had found out.

The web of deceit had been spun, cast wide and Insect Code now could capture its prey in a sticky mess.

BEAR'S DEBRIEF

Intelligence – insects gather lots of information. Honey Bees wiggle to pass on that information locally to other bees. Humans though take vast amounts of information and pass on to others using their own technologies using verbal and other means of communication.

"That was a tremendous success Bear", congratulated the head of Insect Code.

"Have a look here to see what we have done with your information."

He brought some images up onto the screen. These were quite familiar for him although had been adapted carefully.

He quickly flicked through the images. His final one was shown first with the completed plan.

"You have done a remarkable job Bear. Here's what we have made this sketch into."

Up next came a fully three-dimensional rotating image. By adjusting various controls, the head was able to zoom into the building through the doors and navigate through the various rooms. Bear had downloaded from his memory all he knew to the various forensic scientists who then took the detail to create the detailed plan.

"Now, Bear", he continued, "you've not seen this all yet and we'd like to walk you through what we think it was like. How's your memory of it all now?"

Bear replied, "My memory of it all seems quite clear. I think I told the guys most of the stuff already. I'm happy to double check it all though."

The head then took the controls slowly moving from a distance through the main door, past the funnels into the laboratory. He could clearly make out the walls, the doors, the various computers and the machinery.

"Hold on a moment", interrupted Bear. "I've just thought about the electrical supply needed for the site. It's a big place and I can't remember where the energy came from. I don't think there were any obvious generators, no sounds of pumps or anything. Are there solar panels on the roof, above where I could see?"

"We don't think so Bear. It's so far from anywhere that laying a cable would have been an extortionate thing to do. We think that they must have some solar panels, but ones that are disguised to look like greenery. We couldn't pick up anything with our overhead satellite imagery. It all looks clearly like some camouflage. Perhaps there's some new development in solar powered technology that we're just not knowing about."

"There are some other technologies out there that are cheap and simple to use to generate electricity. Is the stream dammed somewhere for a hydroelectric scheme or are there ground heat pumps in use?" Bear suggested.

"Do you want me to go back and have a further look?" Bear wanted to go back. "There was so much to see and do there. So many insects to study and detail to study."

"It's very risky. They know you now and they would be very suspicious if you had another nose about. Saying all that though, does it really matter where their energy is coming from?"

Bear thought back to some of his military days: "we always went for the energy supplies first, the generators and fuel dumps, that sort of thing. Once we'd knocked out those items the target places would be easier to hit."

"Remember", said the head, "we're not a military establishment and we're not totally sure of the best plan forwards to tackle this place. We've a couple of ideas to start coming up with some plans. We could simply wipe the place out. That would be easy. It would generate a load of attention though."

"We've thought about taking down the energy supply too, but as you've just said we don't know how or where it's coming from yet. We've tried hacking into their systems, but they are very secure as far as we can tell."

"It looked like there was some finger print recognition and voice recognition going on", said Bear. "When I was taken into the lab and Bill was on the computer, he seemed to say some words just as we arrived, maybe he was just talking to himself or maybe he had some sophisticated methods of interacting with his computer."

It had long been known that using a keyboard and mouse was quite an inefficient method of accessing a computer. Sixty words a minute typing is not a lot compared to one hundred and fifty words a minute dictating. Voice could also be used to control various functions on the screen and use of inflection was becoming increasingly important. Typing and speech combined would enable a fast entry system if the trained brain could cope with the multi-modal user interface. Eye gaze technology had been developed a few years ago and had virtually overtaken the need for a mouse. Just look at something and say a command and a whole new world opened.

"You are probably right Bear. It seems that this organisation is a well-funded one and full of clever technology people. I hasten to call them geeks, but probably that's what they are. Guys using toys to cause significant destruction in the world. We've geeks here too don't forget, but our staff are here for a much more ethical cause."

"So, what other plans do you have?" Bear asked.

"We're considering targeting the machine itself, but now we don't have information on when it's being used, when it's been protected by the guards, or if at all. When you were there you said, the machine wasn't on. It could be the machine was down for maintenance or the schedule was for use some other time." The head was pondering some ideas.

"Right, I think we've got the plan for the next stage. We need to know more about when the machine is active and when are the guards out and about patrolling the area. That sort of thing."

"That sounds a good plan." said Bear. "Could Martina be of use in the next stage?"

"Probably would be right Bear. Bill and his cronies know you, so someone different would arouse less suspicion. We could drop her in there for a few days. She's got good enough survival skills to last some while and she's crafty enough to hide away safely. It seems that the guards aren't too clever but are a little jumpy. Maybe Bear you could spend some time with her detailing everything you've found out so far?"

"Sure, no problem", agreed Bear.

"I'm pleased we've got something agreed now." The head seemed to settle now having found a new course to move forwards.

GRASSHOPPER

Grasshopper – an insect renowned for communicating by vibrating its hind legs against its body. These insects can be camouflaged and then jump and glide some considerable distance often showing distracting colours

Martina had her head phones on again. These were large and seemingly cumbersome items, but also considered a fashion item. She was deep in the beat and humming gently as she went about her chores at home. Her home was on the twelfth floor of a tower block and she had analysed every exit and escape route from all the rooms.

The lift – an obvious challenge for an escape as she would have to wait for the lift to come up, she wouldn't know who was in the lift and anyone could be waiting for her as she exited. Perhaps the escape hatch on the roof of the lift would work for a way out. She'd seen too many movies where that method worked, but her lift wasn't the same design. Escape wasn't really something to be considered in modern lifts.

The stairs – a good route as she could go up or down or leave at any level. The stairs were bare and very noisy so unless she padded her way down she'd be given away.

The window – well it could be done. She'd need her wings close by to glide from the veranda. She always kept them close by her bed. The wings were like that of a Grasshopper. Most of the time they were collapsed, compact and folded away. They could be spread wide for a long glide path. She hoped she'd never have to use them for a descent.

The music was good. She felt a connection and an empathy with the style. It had good rhythm, interesting harmonies and a varied set of musical hooks throughout. There was too much of this simply manufactured stuff about, a simple beat, monotonous verses and poor singing styles. Too many copy cats instead of new and exciting styles. Each to their own maybe, but she was more discerning.

Martina had been picked to work with Insect Code because of her mastery over the music, the soundscapes and her agility. She was an adventurer and had often used wings when sky diving like a flying squirrel. She would have no problem throwing on her jump suit right now and gliding down to the park below. That gave her a sense of freedom and she loved living in a tower block because of this. A ground dweller could fly nowhere without going up first.

As she efficiently tidied up she had the thoughts of jumping from the building. It gave her a warm glow, a comfortable place for her to be and free.

*

Martina sat at her mixing desk. It consisted of a large array of sliders and switches, all on a virtual touch screen. A human restriction was to have only two hands and ten fingers to control the sound streams. She was adept though and fully in control.

The sound system was linked to a powerful computer and gave out a very high definition sound. She loved to mix noises, sounds and any inspiration she'd obtained when in the field. Today's hook was a forest population sound scene that built up and died down with the emotion of the music.

Her computer pinged with a message. Although pop up messages often distracted people, she was such a good multi-tasker that she could read a message briefly and get back to work without much interruption.

Ping went another message from the same person. She knew this would be a day of pings. Perhaps she needed to turn off the computer or answer a few and be done with a few messages.

Again, it went ping and this was the third message from Insect Code. It must be important as Insect Code was a very secure organisation and rarely sent out messages. She opened the first message fully. It contained a photograph of a Grasshopper. This was of little surprise to her as she was used to insect pictures from Insect Code. It was usual also for several emails to be sent so that she would need to piece together the details to formulate a full message. It was part of their security.

The Grasshopper was a lovely looking specimen. It was long and slender with a rich variety of patterns and mottling. This was all part of its camouflage. There was no sign of the vibrant wings tucked away. The hind legs were thick and muscular ready for a launch. Although large they were excellently controllable. They could vibrate their legs with precision to make a suitable noise.

The second message was a request for a digital app, something to record sounds, process them and them transmit them. This she was passionate about. Taking noises, manipulating them and using digital technology to enhance and cause an emotional response.

She knew she would not have much time or chance to digest the information.

There was a loud rap at the front door. Three knocks. She jumped despite having her high-quality head phones on. This was surprise as she was twelve floors up and there was a secure door entry system. There were tricks to entering buildings with door entry such as following someone else in, but this building had a concierge.

Her suspicions had been aroused and she knew what to do. She had a kill switch close at hand and powered down all the machinery rapidly. In a few seconds it was all quiet and importantly secure. No one could gain entry to her systems. Finger print recognition was a given, but the voice recognition patterns for her voice were clever and impenetrable. Under duress her voice would not let her gain entry. It would take a specific set of voice levels for the system to recognise her.

She was deft and padded across to the security system for the flat door. It was a double door system; double security. There were cameras installed. There was an obvious camera, one to show the person at the door they were being watched. In reality, it was the array of other cameras that did the job. There was an infra-red camera and one that could detect ultraviolet. There were various tools to help identify if there was a genuine caller or not. It sounded paranoid of her. Insect Code had convinced her that there were risks to her special job with them.

She flicked the security systems on and could immediately see there were three women there. They all looked strong and agile, although all dressed in a power suit. She knew, she just knew there was about to be trouble.

It was time to jump from the building.

She knew the visitors would have been watching her flat somehow. Perhaps from the tower block on the other side of the block. Perhaps the concierge had been compromised. Now wasn't the time to analyse that. There would be time later. She knew if they'd gained entry so far it wouldn't be long before they'd be able to enter her flat. The weakest point to any system was by the front door.

She breathed rapidly and focused. Her back pack was now on. Veranda doors slid open effortlessly and soundlessly ready for her to jump.

*

Sixty minutes earlier a small team had seen Martina was in her room. They had been in a flat on the opposite side of the block to Martina's building. They had powerful vision equipment. With hawk like enhancements they could see through the thick veiled net curtains. One of the team made a poor joke about "Annette Curtains" or something similar. It was distracting and irrelevant to the current situation.

They'd seen Martina enter her room and start her chores. It hadn't taken her long. Being a tidy person and doing chores regularly was her philosophy on it all. She'd then started her computer system. The team didn't know what that was all about. Their task was to get Martina, nothing more and nothing less. "Get her and bring her back", they'd been told. They didn't know why and just got on with the job.

It was easy to assume the glowing lights were from her computers to enable her to do her Insect Code business. They were right in many ways, but the music system would probably fool anyone.

"OK team let's go". They collected their things, a few bags and tucked away their weaponry. Each carried a different tool for the job. An electric stun device for disarming, handcuffs for securing and chemicals to break down any door and lock. The Taser had been inspired by an electric eel. Take a high voltage to stun an opponent, but not to kill it. The handcuffs were make from a silken material. This was immensely strong, soft enough to not cause damage and light weight. It would be thrown around a pair of wrists quickly and securely. They'd been a huge enhancement compared to traditional metal cuffs.

The chemicals were highly corrosive and were a cocktail of gel beads each with different properties. On contact with a surface the bead's outer casing would readily dissolve and release the stronger substances inside. Today they would be used to destroy the hinges of various doors. There was always a gap along the edge of a door that chemicals could seep through to destroy the door frame. Often the gap was simply filled with foam to expand and contract as the door moved open or closed.

The team moved swiftly down the stairs making little sound. Hard shoes in the stark stairwell would draw attention too readily. They moved round the back of the tower block along the alleyway and across the block to the back of Martina's tower block. At the back of the building was a service entrance. There was a flood of Closed-Circuit Television systems. This team though were prepared and released a handful of mini-drones. Each would locate the cameras by their infra-red emissions.

The drones climbed well above the highest point of the cameras' views and came down on top of them. Anyone watching the footage would only see a slight movement of the cameras. The wind would also make a slight movement too and would not be noticed.

Once secured in place on top of the cameras they filmed a few seconds of the scene. Then they tapped into the electronics of the cameras and started to playback the recorded video. The security staff or the recordings would show nothing of the next activity.

*

She stood for a moment on the veranda, listening, observing. There was a little wind tonight. There were no other noises at the front door. That was suspicious. If she was wrong and there was not trouble, then all she achieved was a fun flight down from the twelfth floor. She gently closed the sliding doors and locked them from the outside. They would have no clue where she'd gone. They would destroy her possessions, but they didn't matter to her.

She looked around ensuring familiarity with her surroundings. There seemed nothing amiss. No unfamiliar vehicles, no suspicious people. It was all just looking normal, but the presence of the three women was nagging on her mind.

It was about time to go. She reassured herself she was doing the right thing.

*

The team rapped on the door again. They knew that no answer now meant they'd been rumbled. No answer.

The tall team member who carried the delicate chemical pouch stepped forwards and started to crack open the chemicals and eased them down the door hinge side.

"Come on", encouraged one of the others.

"OK, it takes a little time. Just wait..." she replied

"Shhhh", soothed one of the others. "Don't arouse suspicion remember".

The chemicals dripped a little onto the carpet and immediately fizzed. A Venus fly trap had some similar properties to these chemicals, which were packed full of enzymes and potent digesters. Those had been altered in the lab to eat away at various metals and plastic substances.

The door frame started to bubble away a little. A small stream of steam or other vapours rose up. Soon the door was able to be moved a little. It would just be a minute more.

A door clicked along the corridor. Three sets of eyes opened a little, ears sensing detail. They didn't want collateral damage.

There was no more sound. What was the noise, who knows? Focus on the task.

The door soon gave way. They had to work together to ease the door to the floor silently and avoiding the chemicals. They'd practiced this enough times and had plenty of close shaves. The suction devices worked well. This time it was a perfect manoeuvre.

*

Go! She jumped. Pushed off hard from the ledge, enough to be away from the building. Head first, arms out for stability and then click wings open.

She fell rapidly, and it took a few floors before she got control. A small motor started immediately on the jump and propelled her a little. It would burn only for twenty-five seconds, enough to gain some height and travel a few blocks away.

Her wings spread efficiently. A Grasshopper might have blue or red vibrant colours to scare away predators, but Martina's were black. Dark so as not to be seen and absorbent of infra-red and ultra-violet light.

She flew for those twenty-five seconds with ease. First would be a quick turn around her own tower block to get out of immediate view, off the busy road and along a quiet side street. This route had been carefully planned but never executed until today.

*

The team went in low and fast. They spread out, searching. A low profile was important, but the biggest give away was the light streaming in through the open doorway which they had just gome through. Maybe they should have killed the lights in the corridor. They couldn't have thought of everything.

They couldn't find her. Where was she? All the doors were locked. Had she left in the moments from when they left their vantage point to arriving at her door?

The team's vital mistake was to have not left someone in watch from the other tower. They would not have believed what Martina did.

"Damn", one of them exclaimed.

*

The motor stopped and she immediately slowed and continued gliding.

*

When she had jumped, she had released a little creature. It was much like a dragonfly. Sleek and importantly fast. It would not attract any attention from anyone as dragonflies were frequent in the city, especially at this time of year. There were lots of parks with suitable habitat nearby.

The dragonfly moved fast and delivered its message within twenty-five minutes. Martina's flat had been compromised. A secret insect code had been sent.

*

She had good control of her winged suit and cruised across to the nearby park. It was a park with a large open space with enough room to land. The park was empty. That was a risk that had to be taken, was the park full of nosey residents or empty. Tonight, though it was empty.

She landed gently and tucked her wings away. It had been a successful flight.

*

Insect Code got the message, decoded it and acted immediately. A crew was sent to Martina's tower block. Blues and twos all the way. They would no doubt be too late. Insect Code hoped that she'd got away successfully. They knew someone had found out about Martina's work to destroy Bio-Insect Oil's work.

They arrived and streamed upstairs. It was twelve flights and no hassle for the authorities. They arrived on the scene to find the front door compromised. There were no signs of the intruders, they had gone. The place was empty. All the electronics were off, the place was tidy. Not the usual destruction from a burglar. This was as surprise.

Where though was Martina?

*

She was safe now. On the ground and walking swiftly to Insect Code. It would take her twenty minutes to get there with a quick ride in the subway.

At Insect Code's door, she gained entry readily. They were waiting for her. A lot of questions to be asked. She knew nothing. What had happened? Who were these people? She was reassured to know she'd made the right decision to glide away from her flat once she was told about the destroyed front door.

All the Closed-Circuit Television footage had already been analysed and there was no trace of anybody breaking in. This was a clever organisation that had infiltrated. It was now a more pressing need to infiltrate back.

ORTHOPTERA

Orthoptera – planes have fixed wings, helicopters have rotating wings, but despite their meaning of "straight wings", insects like Grasshoppers have a very flexible and versatile set of four wings for agility and speed

It was the class room again. Martina was very familiar with it now. It was now her home as her flat had been compromised.

"OK class today it's about Orthoptera and specifically Caelifera." The teacher said. "So, tell me something about these. What do you know?"

This was an area Martina had grown to know and emulate. "Grasshoppers", she said.

"These are insects..."

"Obviously, insects", interjected Oliver.

Martina ignored him and carried on. "These insects have strong hind legs, long slender bodies and are vegetarian. They are generally camouflaged and evade predators by leaping into the air, spreading a distracting set of wings and are able to glide away rapidly".

"Yeah, yeah, we know", scoffed Oliver.

"The males of the species that call rub their hindlegs on a series of pegs along their body. The arrangement of the pegs causes different vibrations, different tones and rhythms. Some females vibrate too".

"I bet they do", said Oliver.

"Shut it Oliver", retorted Martina.

"Yes, that's the ticket", the teacher continued. "We're going to find out a bit more about these noises. Martina, we know you can glide like a Grasshopper from the other day. We're going to use some of your knowledge here to work out a plan to encode some data."

Bear looked a little confused. "What are we going to be doing this time?", he sounded frustrated. "We've done various things already. Grasshoppers yeah might be crunchy and tasty, but really how are these going to help?"

"You'll see, you'll see."

"First, we'll listen to a few sounds", the teacher said as he tapped the triangle symbol on his tablet.

Throughout the classroom, a loud rasping noise was heard. It repeated several times. The tones were the same each time.

"Tell me about the noise", he asked.

Martina was well tuned into this and could readily analyse various streams of noise. It was a good skill to hear a whole set of music or sounds to get a big picture, then to dissect the noise into various separate streams. This was something akin to listening to a grand opera and then being able to isolate the sounds from one section, or even one instrument.

"I think", she said, "that there are a few different pitches and rhythms. A high-pitched tone probably for short distances and the lower ones for sending messages further.

"She's just hearing things", chortled Oliver.

The teacher continued, "It's a complex array of signals. We're only just starting to understand them. They seem to tell the females about virility, territory, strength and the wing size. All important for evolution and continuation of the to the next generation".

*

Bear remembered his time drawing the Butterflies, the Obtulates, and had a flash back to sitting there in front of the enemy base. He recalled the few Grasshoppers about him. It had been a warm and sunny day and the Grasshoppers were quite active. He knew enough to know that different species probably had different tones and rhythms. He remembered having to brush off one from his arm. He was daydreaming instead of listening to his lesson.

*

"Martina, we need your expertise here to encode some data to emulate the Grasshopper noises. We'll not tell you what data is to be encoded yet. Will you be up for that?"

This was excellent, just what she could get her teeth into.

"My work station though is in my flat and I can't go there to get it".

"No worries", he replied, "we've got it. We managed to get all the bits you'll need. We've run some diagnostics and found its all safe. Don't worry, nothing has been compromised".

"It's only me though that can log in?" She said back in a puzzled way.

"There's always a back door", he replied.

*

Martina spent the next day and night analysing some Grasshopper sounds. She had been given a dozen to work with and told these would be the ones from the next mission site. She wasn't sure how someone would have got the sound recordings, especially high fidelity ones like these. All she knew was Bear had visited the place already. Insect Code wouldn't tell her all the details, only what she needed to know.

She got absorbed into her work and felt at one with the tools at hand. There was a strong connection between her sound manipulation and her positive emotions. She loved a challenge too.

The Grasshopper noises were a little complex. To the human ear, they were repeated and simple, but using the powerful analysis she had at hand there were variations. These subtle changes in the tone and timbre must mean something. What though she did not know.

This was her hook now to developing something clever. She would extract the base noise, the simple sounds the human ear could interpret and use this as a carrier signal for any extra code. In some ways like an encoded system, but the cleverness here was that it was a natural sound, something from nature which would raise little suspicion in the field.

It didn't take long to run up an app to encode some written data amongst some pre-recorded Grasshopper sounds. The trick in the field would be to pretend that the sounds were being recorded live. The intention was for the sound files to be transmitted openly and be intercepted. Once listened to though they would arouse no suspicion. Just a set of weird people recording Grasshopper sounds. It was all an illusion.

GRASSHOPPER DESCENT

Moth defences – some Moths fall from the sky in a controlled manner when they hear a predator such as a bat echolocating them. They must know when the ground is approaching otherwise an evasive fall would end up with certain death

She was dropped. She fell rapidly downwards, fast and direct. The ground quickly approached. It was another descent and it exhilarated her. She had been dropped quite low and the freefall had been all too brief. The rush of the wind, the feeling of danger and out of control got her going every time.

Snap. Her wings opened, and she slowed gaining some control. She brought her flight angle up a little to slow down further. Now she could see the ground layout clearly below. There were several suitable landing sites. It was time to decide and quickly. Getting a landing wrong here meant crashing into the trees and that wouldn't be a pretty sight.

Martina's Grasshopper wings worked well. She landed safely and gently. Perfect.

There was no one about. It was a lucky strike as Bio-Insect Oil's site had several patrols about. She had to fly in the light and land in the light. It would have been too dangerous otherwise.

Quickly she rustled up the wings and got out her entomological equipment. Today's mission was unusual and very quirky. She had been working intensively to master the encoding for her digital recordings she was about to make. First it was surveillance, then came the trickery.

She walked for some time in the direction planned. She'd made a mental map of her objective and carried a map that showed none of the Bio-Insect Oil encampment. The map in her hand was an old map and deliberately so to fool the enemy if she was caught. She was innocent, a collector of Grasshopper sounds. She hoped she would not need to play the innocent card. Time would tell, time to focus.

The trek was straight forward. There were several tracks and simple paths with various glades opening out into brief vistas. There were also wide expansive grasslands. She knew immediately there would be plenty to study here. Lots of Grasshoppers, Butterflies, Crickets, Moths and lots of other bugs and insects. It could be such a distracting place for her with so much sound about.

She found one lovely meadow and decided it was time to record some chirping insects. She took out her especially locked down smart device. It had been made to resemble a recording unit with limited functionality. A slightly updated Dictaphone. A few buttons to tap to record, playback and view any recordings. It had a send button. Straight forwards, to send the recordings nothing more. That was the spin.

The secret behind the device, despite its simple nature, was to encode the data she would be collecting in a while and send that data back to Insect Code. Vital data to the conclusion of this mission.

*

As she sat in the meadow there were several Grasshoppers about. Not as many as would have been expected from a lush meadow such as the one she was sitting in. There was a rich variety of grasses and flowers. The flora was diverse. There were a few sights and sounds indicating that there were several insects about. A few Butterflies flitted about and a few occasional chirrups close by.

"A damaged landscape indeed", she thought out loud. "So few insects about". She was feeling sad about it all. "Oh well, best get on and try to get a few Grasshoppers to record."

She set about her business with a net in hand and a pot at the ready to capture any Grasshoppers that she found. It took her a little time to search the area, to track some of the sounds, but she managed to capture a few insects after a while.

The first Grasshopper was a small one, an early stage nymph. She hoped it would make some noises for her. This might be tricky as captured insects didn't always behave in captivity as they would in the wild.

This insect was mottled green; she had seen that the wings were a bright red, a big flash of colour when the wings spread open. The body was fine and slender, and the patterning detailed. The interest in insects was all about the detail, the patterns, the colours, the habits and their characters. She remembered her flight down and her resemblance of a Grasshopper, just like the one at hand.

This Grasshopper was lively and wanting to escape from the pot. A trick was to fool the insect into believing the sun was behind a cloud or it was night time, so she quickly placed it in her bag out of the direct sunlight.

This insect calmed down readily in the darkness, but then it wouldn't start making noises. Perhaps it was too young or hadn't learnt what the noises it could make meant in the world. She didn't know. She liked to think about these things a little, maybe she could discover something new and interesting. It was all about observation.

Martina let the little insect go into the grass. It quickly jumped away and disappeared.

It took a little time before she found another Grasshopper. This time it was a larger one with beige colouration. She had seen the wings as it flew and they also were a very vibrant, like the first one. Its eyes were scanning the area, intently inspecting the environment and what was happening to it. It was beige to blend in with the browning grass stems.

The insect made a few brief chirrups with his hind legs vibrating rapidly. It was a thrilling little noise and evocative of this peaceful meadow. The noises grew in intensity and length. This was a good sign for getting a few recordings done.

She brought out her recording device, the secret smart device. She pressed the on button and the screen came to life straight away, none of the waiting that frustrated users of technology in the past. The first screen was the recording screen. It would take some secret entry method to get at the inner workings of the phone.

She took a few recordings and played them back. The Grasshopper was intrigued by the played back sound. This must mean that she had captured a good quality sound with all the relevant frequencies and the Grasshopper here reacted appropriately to the played back sounds. She took some notes and a couple of photographs, packaging all the information together. The first step in her deception was now secured in the device. The Grasshoppers get captured in a pot and then released; their sounds are captured in the phone and then sent into the airways.

She took some time to find more Grasshoppers. It took longer than would have been expected, but she persevered. Studying nature was not a predictable thing and in this forest, it was proving more challenging than elsewhere. She knew some of the reason why but had to keep that quiet.

*

She was approximately five kilometres from the main site. She had crossed the vehicle track a few times and had tried to keep to the paths, primarily so that she could find the most insects to study. Also, this helped her keep a lower profile without raising suspicion.

At one point her path crossed the track, which had fresh tyre treads in the mud. Without warning a Land Rover pulled along the track. The undergrowth must have been so dense, and she had been concentrating too much on the ground around her that it nearly knocked into her.

The vehicle skidded to a halt and the guards jumped out.

Her adrenaline pumped through her body, and her heart rate increased rapidly. She mustn't forget her training in dealing with threatening people.

"Hey, watch it", shouted one of the guards. "We nearly ran you over."

Another guard interjected, "are you OK lady?"

"Yes, erm fine, just shocked how you came so fast from the forest."

"Sorry about that", said the second guard.

"That's OK", she replied, "continue on your way. You nice guys look like you are in a hurry."

"We sure are. Our delivery is arriving shortly and we're low on beer."

With that they jumped back into the Land Rover and pulled away swiftly. Martina was left a little stunned. Surely, they would have asked her more questions. Maybe they were as dim-witted as she had been told they were.

*

As the Land Rover jumped along the track, the guards continued their excitement about the delivery. They had been radioed only a few minutes ago from Bill to say that the delivery would be there soon. It was a lonely existence in the field with just the four men about and any contact with the outside world was welcome.

"Should we say anything to Bill about the lady?" said one of the guards.

"No, let's not bother. She looked harmless enough and anyway she was nowhere near where we need to protect. Let's just forget it".

They carried on at a pace too eager to think any more about see-ing a lady in the middle of the forest many kilometres from any-where. The pull of beer was too strong. Martina had been right that these guards were not very clever at their job.

*

Martina had become a little scared some while after the brief encounter as she thought about what could have happened. She needed to keep her head down now and be more vigilant. A lit-tle less listening to nature sounds and a little more listening out for human made noises.

She carried on her journey. She did not have too far to go now, but the terrain was becoming more challenging. She had de-cided to walk along the edge of the vehicle track. She had been told that there was only one vehicle on the site. She had seen that it had now driven away from her at speed. This told her the quickest way to get to the site without needing her navigation equipment; a simple bit of tracking and initiative. Also, she had a clear view along the track and could hear more readily now. If the vehicle came back, she could dive into the undergrowth quickly.

The track was lined with a diverse array of flora. The trees were lush and tall. A few large Butterflies descended from the tree tops to nectar on the ground-based flowers. They glided down and with delicate control landed deftly on the flower heads. This reminded her of her journey to the ground from the Coccinelle earlier.

After an hour's trek she came across the site of Bio-Insect Oil's machinery. It was quite large and imposing with a wide-open space in front of it. There clearly were no insects or birds about in this area. The destruction was evident by the absence of animal life.

She did not come out into the open to do her studies. This would be far too obvious. She needed a place to hide and to study the movements at the site.

The site was on a hill side and the opposite side of the valley was too far away to be any good for seeing the site close to. There were plenty of tall trees about, so she decided to investigate.

The trees were tall, and their bases had a wide girth. There were plenty of hand holds for her to grip onto. The vines also looked like they would readily support her weight. She found a suitable tree about two hundred metres from the site. It had a direct view of the site and had various lower trees obscuring the lower parts of this tree. This looked suitable for her to make her observation post.

It took her some ten minutes of intense climbing to get to a suitable place. The tree was old and substantial about fifty metres tall. There was much growth around the tree from vines, creepers, orchids and various other plants. She did not want to disturb the flora as it may have made it easier for someone to follow her tracks. She had been careful along the track not to leave many boot prints.

She had settled down at a large branch that had ample room for her to sit on comfortably. The mosses and other tree hugging plants made for a soft seat to sit on.

She was in place now and could start her observations. The observer doesn't want to be observed.

*

It was now midday and the sun was quite high making for a warm day. It would continue to get warmer until it was nearly dusk. She now needed to record the movements at the site. She had been told that the Moths were collecting information about when the machine; when it was working, but this needed to be backed up with information about people movements, numbers of guards and any vehicular activity.

She knew that the guards had come back and that there was a delivery due shortly from what they had said. She had not heard any other vehicle arriving or seen any evidence of a delivery.

She heard a humming noise from behind the site. It was approaching quite fast, but she could not tell what it was. As the sound got quite loud she saw that it was a quad-copter, quite a large one. These machines had developed a lot over the past twenty years from rudimentary remote-controlled devices to these now fully autonomous craft. They could lift a substantial weight and carry items for quite some distance to precise locations even hovering to dispatch and obtain goods as required.

This drone was carrying some cargo under its belly which meant it could not land straight away. It came to the side of the building and lowered down with precision. Once the cargo had touched the ground it was released, and the craft moved away a little to some sort of platform. It looked as if the platform was a helicopter landing pad although it was much smaller. The craft landed and powered down. A small probe inserted itself into the craft. She thought this must be a refuelling system or recharging system. Perhaps taking a form of nectar using its own proboscis.

Two of the guards came out of the building and took away the cargo. That must be the beer and the essential items. She didn't consider beer to be essential, but guessed these guys were here for many weeks back-to-back and needed something to entertain themselves. It really didn't matter. The guards were distracted and that was helpful.

After only thirty minutes the craft started up and flew away quickly. It was not taking any cargo back with it. Perhaps it would be back later; she hoped to find out.

She had her recording device open and by tapping the right coded entry got into hidden areas. She entered all her observation data and quickly closed the hidden screen away to reveal the recording screen again. If she was caught she didn't want to have to explain the hidden screen to anyone as that would compromise her mission.

There was much time when nothing happened. It was tedious work and with little wildlife about she had limited things to focus upon. There were only a few insects and birds.

She carried on eating her various energy bars and had enough water for two whole days. In her back pack she also carried some water purification tablet and a filter. This would enable her to drink for up to a week if required. Her mind wandered a little. Perhaps she could sneak into the building and find some other food, perhaps from the next drone delivery. What though if the next delivery was just beer? That would be disappointing. She would then have her cover blown. Maybe not a good idea. She needed to stay focused.

The building started to gently emit a low-pitched noise. It wasn't very loud, but audible enough, especially for someone so skilled in sound analysis. She became intrigued.

The giant funnels at the front of the building looked as if they were moving. She wasn't sure if it was an illusion or it really was moving. She had time and was content to keep watching what was happening.

After a short while her sense of smell twitched a little, undetectable at first. She had got used to the various smells of the forest, some sweet, some musty and some sharp. Just now though there was a different smell in the air. It reminded her of some of the laboratory work and of men. It was a strange combination. She remained confused, but only a little. Her senses were awake now trying to work out what was going on.

There was definitely activity in the air now. There were various Moths fluttering about searching for something. They spiralled in the direction of the funnels. There were other insects too, but she was too far away from the machine to know what they were.

She realised that she was smelling the pheromones from the machine. The way the machine was attracting insects to it must be with airborne pheromones. She must have been smelling the pheromones and her poor smell sense must have been triggering a smell memory from the laboratory, something subliminal. Men must also be letting out a subtle smell too, although she knew some that weren't so subtle in the smell stakes. These weren't sweaty smells but something quite different activating quite a different part of her brain.

She remembered her mission and became focused. Her job was to note down any events. This was definitely an event to take note of in her smart device. She noted the start time and the time of her observations, all coded into in the handheld device.

The insect life was increasing in number. It sickened her to see a stream of insects pouring into the machine. They definitely weren't coming out of that machine alive. Whatever it was at the end of the funnel was trapping them. She presumed they were being killed and made into some sort of oil. That's all she knew about the process. To see it first-hand though was awful.

She now had her own smell memory of this event. If she smelt it again she knew it would be the machine working.

The machine kept going for four hours. The humming then stopped. The insects had stopped arriving some while ago, which she duly noted.

It was time to send some data away. She had developed the coding to use the Grasshopper signals as a disguise for the data she was about to package up.

The Grasshopper noises would be left un-encoded so that anybody receiving her secret signals would hear simply Grasshoppers. Insect Code had hoped this would mean any listener would simply disregard the signal.

She tapped 'send' once the movements she had observed were encoded into the Grasshopper noises. The data went quickly. In some ways, she hoped her signal would be intercepted just to see if her system was working or not. Maybe she would never find out.

*

Inside the site, Bill was bored. He'd worked the machine lots of times now and felt he'd seen everything, done everything and experienced everything. He was fiddling with his computer, just looking at data, nothing more.

His computer bleeped, and a small icon changed from green to red. It was a small icon to say that he'd picked up a signal that hadn't originated from their computers or from Bio-Insect Oil. Could he be bothered to find out more about it? He wasn't sure.

He felt on balance though that he should investigate a little. He didn't have anything else to do; not whilst the machine wasn't active anyway.

He tapped away at the screen and opened the signal. It was a digital file containing sounds. It was a simple compressed sound file. Nothing unusual in that. He opened the file in his media player. His computer could readily decompress the file.

He heard a familiar sound. It was the sound of a Grasshopper calling. There were many different types of Grasshopper around this site, but he'd heard fewer and fewer recently. It didn't cause him any trouble, it was just a simple recording of Grasshoppers.

He was so tired and bored that he couldn't really think much about the sounds and if it meant just a recording or something else. 'Who cares?', he thought.

One of the guards came in at that time when Bill was playing the recording.

"What are you playing now?" He inquisitively asked.

"It's just a recording I've intercepted of some Grasshoppers. I guess there may be someone out there recording these things." Bill said without much care.

"That reminds me," the guard said, "we nearly knocked over someone on the track today. A red headed lady."

Bill was a bit more alert now.

"Did you bring her in then?" Bill said. "What was she doing? Where did you find her?"

"Oh, about five kilometres down the track. She looked innocent enough. We didn't stop long as we were back for the delivery."

"Didn't I tell you to report everything?" Quizzed Bill.

"Well, err, yes I suppose. She didn't look anything much."

"What was she doing? Did you find that out at least?"

"No we didn't. We had the delivery to attend to." He gave an assertive reply.

Bill sighed. It was like talking with animals at times and not getting much of a reply.

"Right, get everyone here pronto."

The guard scampered out to get the others. It didn't take long for them to come back.

"You three need to buck your ideas up. You've all seen another person out there and done nothing about it." Bill didn't give them a chance to reply. "Right we're going to up the watch and you're going to report to me every hour now."

"OK", they all chorused together.

Bill now had a think about what it was all about. He'd seen a guy collecting Butterflies, a mysterious woman and he'd found a recording of Grasshoppers. Was there any connection? He thought he'd put down his thoughts to Henry his boss.

He typed up a message with the details. It was a good way for him to get his thoughts organised. He tapped send and the data went. He thought the data went. He didn't know about the Dragonfly interrupting the data stream.

He'd hoped that there would be a reply in the morning with some advice as to what to do. In the meantime, he would just have to be vigilant for the site and to get a proper control of the guards.

*

One of the guards was stationed at the entrance of the building all through the night. The lights of the building were left on to aid the security. The guard sat there all night being vigilant. He didn't want to hear the wrath of Bill again.

Once he caught sight of a glint in the distance. Perhaps something blowing in the wind or one of those glowing bugs. It only happened once. He didn't do anything about it.

*

Martina had kept using her binoculars to see what was going on in the building. It was all quiet. She had seen that a guard had been stationed outside now. She hadn't expected this, and with her paranoia felt that her message had been intercepted and the guards had become suspicious. She'd wondered too why the guards hadn't asked her more questions earlier when they came across her on the track. They hadn't come out to investigate to see if she was still around though.

The guard had looked straight at her at one point when she moved her binoculars down. Perhaps he'd seen a reflection or something from the glass? He continued looking directly at her, but he never moved from his position and never did anything.

Martina remembered to continue to be careful from here. She was very close to the site and at the point of greatest risk of being found by the patrolling guards.

*

She remained in the tree for forty-eight hours. She coped with the lack of movement by small position changes. Her athleticism and yoga helped significantly. She had collated data and sent it regularly. Each time she sent data she checked there were no extra consequences. Maybe her signals had not been detected or intercepted.

The forty-eight hours were up, and she had got the rhythm of the place, the movement of the guards and when the machine was running and what happened to the people. All the data was collated and sent away.

She climbed down from the tree at dusk.. There was still enough light to see with, but not enough light for her to be seen. She now knew the window of time in which she could move about when the guards were busy outside the building or somewhere inside it.

The weather had held for her in the two days of study. There had been no rain storms or strong winds. It seemed quite a peaceful place despite the machine.

She knew the path to take back to her pick-up point. The Land Rover took this track several times a day. She had timed her movements to be there just after the vehicle had come back to its base. It was the least likely time for them to come out again on patrol. Or so she thought.

She trekked fast for thirty minutes to move away from the site efficiently. Her legs were a little stiff from all the sitting about, but soon she was moving swiftly. She heard a vehicle coming. This was unexpected and not within her predicted plan.

The Land Rover swung in behind her and the three guards jumped out. Her instinct was to run. She had no time to dive into the undergrowth and at this particular spot there was a ravine to the one side and a rock face on the other. She was trapped. A few minutes later and she would have been clear.

"So, we meet again lady", one of the guards said. "I think you're coming with us this time."

She was bundled into the Land Rover. She didn't resist as she reminded herself to remain within character. Trying to run away would have meant a great deal of suspicion. The Land Rover revved its engine and brought them at a surprising speed back to the base.

Inside the building, she was taken to a room with a man that she presumed was Bill the entomologist. He wasn't looking very happy.

"Who are you lady?" He barked. "This is not public property?"

"Oh, I'm sorry I thought it was a National Park and free to investigate my Grasshoppers."

"Grasshoppers eh? So, it's you that's been sending Grasshopper recordings about the place?"

"Yes, that's me". She felt a slight redness rising and must quell it.

She dived in with some enthusiasm, "Love the Grasshoppers, such amazing little creatures. Do you know about?"

"Maybe a little", Bill replied, "it's not about me, this is about you. So, what's your name?"

"I'm Martina", she out stretched her hand, but it wasn't taken. Anything to hide the fact she had been spying on these people. She was acting confident. "So, who are you?"

Bill didn't answer her question, although she knew the answer already.

"I can see you've been taking recordings of these creatures." He played one through the speakers of his computer.

"Cool aren't they", she said once it had finished playing.

"Why are you sending these recordings through the air waves?"

"It's just a backup in case I lose my recording device. I'm a bit clumsy you see, and I tend to break stuff."

"You don't look clumsy to me!" he surmised.

"I don't believe you are here studying Grasshoppers Martina. They're not active at night time."

"I know they're not active at night, but dusk is a great time to find out more about them. We know little about these forest Grasshoppers. Do you want me to show you the way I record them? I've a cool little recording gadget I think you'd like."

"Well OK then", he replied.

Martina's bag had been taken off her earlier and searched. She knew that would happen and just kept calm about it. She was given her bag back and she took out the recording device, switched it on and the screen straight away came into the recording section. She had fortunately remembered to come out of the hidden part of the device.

"Just tap the record icon and you record the sounds. It's got an adapted microphone here to record a wider range of frequencies than we can hear. Just tap that stop icon when you are done."

"You can add a photograph or two also. Here I'll show you."

She took the device and snapped a few pics of Bill at his desk. Bill obviously wasn't thinking straight. He shouldn't be letting Martina take photos inside the building.

She flashed the photos at him and quickly showed him a new screen where she could enter some text, times and other useful bits of information.

"Once I'm done," she continued, "I store up a few recordings and then email them away."

"You must have intercepted one of my emails. Sorry to cause you trouble in this. I'm keen just to learn more about these cool little guys. I see you have three cool guys working for you too. They could drive a little better mind you. They nearly knocked me over the other day."

"Yeah they're not very delicate creatures I know." Bill replied.

The guards became a little uncomfortable at that, shuffling

about. She was gaining the upper hand she felt now.

Bill pondered out loud, "A Butterfly collector, a Grasshopper collector. I can't work it out yet. What's going on?"

Martina knew that Bill was talking about her colleague Bear, but she did not let on.

"Look lady you either tell me now what's happening here, or you are going to be in more trouble than you think", he threatened her.

"Hey, don't be like that. I'm only here to record Grasshoppers. You can find me on the web if you like to prove who I am and read my scientific papers on the matter."

Bill backed down a little. "Your story seems good. I'm just not convinced."

"Perhaps your lovely guys could take me in their Land Rover over the ridge, so I can get back to my laboratory quicker. You've delayed me a couple of hours already."

"OK, OK. You're right. I'm sorry to trouble you Martina. Look we're running a business here and don't want any snoopers. It detracts from our work you know."

With that the interview was over. It wasn't as bad as it could have been. Bill wasn't a law enforcer nor was he skilled in the art of questioning. He seemed a clever yet angry person.

She was taken towards the Land Rover. "So where to lady", one of the guards asked? Before she could reply he said, "Just kidding we're not a taxi service. We've been told to take you over that ridge there to help you on your way."

"Can I use the toilet and get some food and water before I go." She threw her water container at the guy who promptly dropped it. A clever little manoeuvre staged to embarrass the guard a little.

"Sure you can, though we don't have a ladies' toilet here." He laughed at his own little private joke.

She took her time and managed to take a few pictures whilst she was away using her smart device. These guys are not really guard's people. Maybe a few extra photographs would help the mission. A free trip inside the building was a boon. She couldn't believe the freedom she had been given considering Bill had tried to give her a grilling about her activities. He had dropped his guard very quickly.

*

The journey over the ridge was as bumpy and uncomfortable as she expected. The driver didn't care much about comfort, he just wanted to get this part of the job done and completed. Maybe he had a beer waiting for him.

"Bye now", the guards said sarcastically to her, "Mind how you go."

Martina had got all the information she needed and more. It had been a breeze to get inside the factory. Now all she had to do was get back to Insect Code and report in.

MARTINA'S DEBRIEF

Multiple defences – camouflage is only as good as the way it blends into the background. Movement can give it all away. Several strategies are sometimes needed to evade detection: colouration, subterfuge and surprising bursts of energy can all work together

"You were lucky Martina." Jacqui had brought Martina directly to her office at Insect Code. "From what you've said your cover was nearly blown."

"I think that Bio-Insect Oil are a poorly run company Jacqui. Look, their machine might be doing the job they set out to do, but their security is pretty useless", Martina said.

"Their guards cannot secure anything. They make so much noise and were easily manipulated. You know they even took me into their building and I could almost wander around freely. When I went to the toilet there, they left me alone. I tried to take a few extra pictures of the internals of the building to help out a bit more. Perhaps they were scared I was a woman and didn't know how to treat me."

"I guess I know what you mean Martina. We have some amazing people work here both men and women." Jacqui replied.

"I know, it's just these guys weren't up to the job and that worked for me." Martina smirked a little.

"Did you get all the things that I sent back to you?" Martina asked.

"Sure, we've got them here. The recordings you did were tremendous. I think the Grasshopper trick worked and we'll have to use that again sometime. They may be on to us though as we've raised their suspicions twice now."

Jacqui continued, "we've started to analyse your data and think we're probably near some conclusions about the site movements already."

There was a sharp rap at the door.

"Come in", called Jacqui. She could see through the glass that it was one of the scientists.

"What have you got for us?", asked Jacqui.

"Hey Martina. How are you?" asked the scientist.

"I'm good. Glad to be back with a mug of coffee." She smiled.

"OK, so we've got all of Martina's data, including the extra photographs you took, now in our lab. It looks like there's a mini factory going on inside that place. Everything is so clearly labelled. This Bill guy seems very organised and fastidious about getting everything in the right place and the right place for everything. We could read all the labels on the things you photographed. Most of the species for the pheromones we could identify were not pest species."

"It was so worthwhile being taken inside the building. I'm glad now that I was caught." She looked very pleased with herself.

"It looks clearly like the site has regular movements with the guards coming and going. Regular means patterns and we can predict, or think we can predict, their movements. We think there will be some shortish time window in which we can disable the site. Most of the time it is running, being maintained or work is going on behind the scenes. We probably need more information about when the machine is running though to ensure we get the disabling of the plant accurate. We want to minimise any collateral damage, if any at all."

"Too right," said Jacqui, "Remember we're here for environmental protection using insects to find a way to help us protect the landscape and the biodiversity."

"Do you think me being taken into the site has had any bearing on the routines much?" asked Martina.

Jacqui replied, "It may do, but trying to understand their personalities, they seem sloppy and likely to fall back into their existing routines. That would just be easy for them. Changing things about could be a headache for them to organise. As you said these guards aren't the cleverest in the box and routine is probably important for them and gives them a little sense of stability in the jungle."

"Probably will just be the same, we think". Said the scientist.

"You've done a great job Martina. We thank you for the efforts. We're glad we didn't lose you out there", said Jacqui.

"No worries Jacqui. It was fun really. Happy to help out."

"We've some more questions for you though. Have a think back a bit more about the lab. Up here you can see some more detail of the lab."

Jacqui pointed up to the screen and there was the three-dimensional interpretation of the site. The tech people had worked tirelessly with Bear and Martina's information to draw up a detailed view of the site.

"Let me give you what we know already", Jacqui was in a thoughtful mode now. "These guys are extracting insects from the forest. You said you 'sensed' something in the air when the insects all got sucked into that machine of theirs. It seems that the things in the air were attracting the insects. They must have been pheromones; organic and volatile chemicals used by females to attract males. It seems surprising them that you, as a female, detected any airborne chemicals".

"That does seem a little odd doesn't it". Martina was racking her brain now for some answers, something to help push this forward a bit. "Well what about considering that it is the female of one specific species that intends to attract the males of the one species. That's the idea, but surely there must be interaction of males from other species with the pheromones. Even if that interaction is just a nod to the smell and gets ignored. Perhaps that's all it was. Perhaps I could just sense that there were pheromones about so beware there are males about."

"Good advice for life Martina", the scientist threw back.

"I was in an area where the concentration and diversity of smells was so great that I could smell them out. Enough for a reaction".

Jacqui replied, "That sounds reasonable. It's like seeing another species, acknowledging it's there, but not doing anything about it. I'm not sure this is going to add much to us. Pheromones as far as I know are a really diverse set of chemicals and we don't have any capability or capacity to analyse any of the smells. We don't even have any pheromones. They are notoriously difficult to capture and retain before they deteriorate. At least we've some strong evidence now that this is the way in which the insects are being attracted into the machine."

"I can feel the chemicals now. My smell memory must be working. Wish I could just put my finger on it all and get some sense of it."

The scientist added, "You'll not get any sense of it. You can consciously process this stuff as it's all subconsciously analysed. You'll just have to let it go".

"So, Martina cast your mind back. Did you see any female insects about?", asked Jacqui.

"I'm not really sure. I was some distance from the site and the insects too small to see. There weren't any that landed near me. The attraction of the machine must have been too strong."

"OK now the drone that you saw", she continued.

"Yes."

"We could track that readily. It's a relatively slow moving and quite noisy device. We've seen where it went to and from. They've set up a series of power stations along the track and other easily accessible places. These power stations simply are charging points for the drone. It lands for 30 minutes, recharges and then goes on. That's all straight forwards."

"You said that the drone brought beer!"

"Yep sure did. That's all the thugs there wanted. I suppose they wouldn't care about much else."

"We agree with that. The cargo though must have had other things in it. Maybe there is a way to sabotage the supply chain. Swap water for vinegar, or pain killers for sleeping pills, or perhaps something to make their chemical factory not work."

"Can't you tell that from what was put on the drone?", Martina thought that would have been obvious.

"Yes, that would have been the case except there are too many of those drones about. They're using a distribution centre that sends out 500 drone flights a day. It's the new way of distributing items doors to door and this particular company is trying it out in with the relatively isolated and inhospitable place around the place we're interested in. We can't possibly tell which cargo is which! It would be a massive task to infiltrate the warehouse."

"I've already downloaded my thoughts on that. All I know is that there was beer. I guess there were other items too. Just too hard to tell."

The scientist interrupted. "We need you to take yourself back there in your mind and recall some detail. Anything might help. Just visualise a little."

Martina relaxed a little, closed her eyes and took a few gentle and deep breaths. This helped her get deep into her mind and recall anything from the site. She recalled the drone, speaking out the details she remembered; it's size, speed, colour and some other details. The cargo was below in a box about 50 centimetres wide, high and deep. The box was just plain.

"OK, keep digging up thoughts. Think inside the building and what you saw. Maybe some packaging would give you clues."

"Just some beer", she replied. "I'm just not getting anything else."

"That's OK Martina", said Jacqui. "Maybe you'll recall some other detail later and send it across."

*

The meeting was over, but she still felt the need to rack her brains. Perhaps in the calm of her sleep she would dream about some important details she had missed before. She kept going over the details she remembered. 'What was the Beer? What was it packaged in? What were the other items? Were they heavy or light?' There were very many things lodged in her head. Perhaps she would find something of relevance.

MOTH

*Moth – an insect, often nocturnal, sometimes diurnal,
often camouflaged, sometimes with vibrant warning
colours, able to fly great distances to find a mate*

"A robot Moth!" Oliver groaned. "What? More crazy ideas. This is getting daft, we've had the flapping Locust and a Butterfly collector."

Oliver had been in the class room with Bear and Martina. He'd found it difficult to take in all the technology and how it would be used. Some mad scientists coming up with some phoney idea.

'Why had he been chosen', he kept thinking, 'why me?'.

"You've done well so far", said that teacher. "You're a good student, just keep it going. We've not much more to do now."

"But, we've been studying these insect things for weeks now", said Oliver. "Can't we do something else". He was sounding so like a teenager now.

"OK, OK", retorted the teacher. "I get it, you're tired, poor thing. Maybe you want this to fail. It's such an important thing we're doing here. You'll see how it all works soon enough. Look we'll get through a few more lessons and then you'll have your fun. You'll see."

Oliver really didn't see. He'd nearly had enough. It had

been wing structures, proboscises, procreating insects, wiggly worms and all sorts of stuff for ages now. It seemed all so irrelevant.

"So, guys", the teacher went on.

"Hey, I'm not a guy, stop saying guys", exclaimed Martina. It seemed that Oliver's mood was getting infectious.

"So, guys AND girls", he over emphasised, "we're going to talk about the robot moth. You'll need to know about this as you may see it out in the field and will have to release a few." The 'have' too caused a small groan from the pupils. They knew what it meant: a new task ahead.

"These creatures are masters of disguise, can fly huge distances just to find a mate."

Oliver sniggered. He really was a teenager at heart and found anything to do with mating amusing. Martina shot him a hard stare, but that had no impact.

"To find a mate the males use these antennae to find their chosen target. A female if you wish. The antennae are large", he showed a few pictures on the screen of moth antennae. They were very intricate, delicate, but amazingly powerful organs able to drive the moth to its own small target. An inspiring aspect of evolution able to change the way the structures grow in response to changing smells and chemicals in the air. Humans have found evolution hard to digest, but always looked at their own timescale, a few decades, rather than the hundreds and thousands of years needed to make big or noticeable changes in populations.

"The little insects can detect a female from over two kilometres away just by smelling her".

Oliver grinned and said, "I've known a few females like that too".

The teacher ignored his comment and Martina rolled her eyes.

"The male moth needs to get to the female before any other. The pheromone the female exudes travels downwind forming a plume shape that covers a huge volume of space. The male can pick up a single pheromone molecule and act on that. He can detect it and know the direction in which it came from."

"Like some sort of radar system", suggested Bear.

"Yes, that's right", the teacher replied. "Radar, but so much more clever and signals are only received rather than been sent out and received back, a one-way radar. They can detect their own species and ignore all other species. The density of pheromones in the air gives the idea of closeness to the female. Once the direction of the plume is known then it's a relatively simple task in the open air to find the female. In a woodland, there are so many obstacles to navigate and the moth is exceptional at finding its way to a successful mating."

"That's amazing", said Martina. "How can it know which direction the pheromone is coming from?"

"An interesting observation Martina. The moth knows the wind direction, it's flying after all and can tell the wind direction by the forces acting on the left and right wings; more wind of the right means turn left a little and head straight into the wind. Also, those antennae I showed you are long and branching. A pheromone landing at the leading end of the left antennae will stimulate the moth to travel in that direction a little. When many pheromone molecules are landing on the antennae a little mental map is generated to pin point the target. Something like having many radar devices in one."

"So, we get all that, but what do we need to do and why are we learning about this moth today?" said Bear.

"Well, you'll need to know how these insects work so that we can accurately track the pheromone signals from the enemy target." Informed the teacher.

"Yes, but why the pheromones? What's that got to do with a military target? We're not chasing female Moths about, are we?" said Oliver.

"In a way, yes you are." The teacher raised an eyebrow. You see the target we'd been discussing previously has been letting out pheromones to attract all the insects from the forest to draw them in and destroy them.

"That's crazy", exclaimed Bear. "Destroying a forest full of insects! Why are they doing that?".

"You see the forest is a huge energy system. Sun shines on the forest and generates herbage, insects feed on the herbage to make proteins and carbohydrates. This upstart of a company is taking all that energy storage and crushing the insects with some fancy process to make oil. They've been selling it as Eco-oil but hiding the truth behind how they are making it. They've been saying it is from a sustainable forest. We've had people out there studying and it's a lie, a whole pack of lies."

"Why do you think it's in such a far-flung place", he continued. "It's an illegal activity and so far, they've destroyed a vast forest area. No insects mean the eco balance is destroyed and the forest gets stifled and eventually will die. It's just not sustainable."

Martina, Bear and Oliver were now listening intently. This part of the saga was putting things together and they could see a little of what they were there for. There were still many questions to be answered. There would be time for some of these later.

The Butterfly task that Bear had done now let him slot into place a small piece of the puzzle. He'd done a good job. When he remembered what he had done he smiled slightly at the thought. An unusual thing for him to do.

Martina had observed great detail from her task. It had been a bit uncomfortable sitting in that tree for two days, but all the information sent back had been well received.

Each member of the team did not know the full detail of each other's tasks. They could piece together some of the information. They'd been instructed to keep things quiet and keep things close to them unless instructed by Insect Code.

*

The Coccinelle was in action again. It purred along the runway and swiftly took off. Tonight, it was in a sleek and very streamlined shape. Its body was compressed and slender. It could fly faster and longer now. The cargo it held on board was calm and in a small compartment at the back of the craft.

The pilot flew directly to near the target area. He would need to put the craft into its stealthiest mode in case it was spotted or tracked in any way.

Once over the target site he reduced the speed down significantly. One of the most vulnerable times for the craft was when the rear door opened and the radar signals from the ground would have the greatest chance of detecting it. The hole though made by the door would be small tonight, just big enough for them to squeeze through.

He slowed the craft and brought the swept wings to the forward position. The speed decreased and the gentle noises from outside the craft subsided further.

In the back of the craft Oliver had been lying down. He was facing the rear of the craft in cramped conditions. His role tonight was to look after the box of delights awaiting to be released for their important and unique mission.

The box contained ten mini robots, each awaiting their instructions. Oliver had his tablet computer to hand and was monitoring their status. There were ten green lights for ten fully functioning Moths ready to be dropped over the Bio-Insect Oil site.

He flicked the screen to access the programming area. He chose the instructions for the insects and started the upload process. It was swift and within thirty seconds all the insects were programmed. He then flicked a switch on the screen to activate them all. His screen buzzed with connections and quickly they were all settled and communicating with each other repeatedly and with him as the main controller.

"One minute to drop point", came Saj's voice gently through Oliver's ear piece. Any sounds projected through the speakers would be more likely to be picked up from the outside as the hull could act as a sounding board. Quieter the better in all things.

Oliver now started to pick out the Moths from their box and arrange them ready for release from the back of the Coccinelle. They acted like Moths crawling with all six legs and moving their antennae about; they were able to interact with the air. These antennae were very large structures and required for the task over the next few days. The antennae were like ferns with one main stem and various branches coming off each side. Each had a vast array of sensors and micro-noses each detecting organic chemicals in the air.

"Twenty...fifteen...ten...", his voice was calm and precise.

The hatch at the back of the craft now opened, just enough to let these Moths be released. Each was the size of his hand, large, but in no way the biggest in the world. Insect Code's hope though was that they would not be seen.

As each one was gently pushed towards the door they started vigorously using their four wings ready for a perfect flight. In nature, these Moths would have to warm up for three to four minutes until their muscles were at the correct temperature.

These robot Moths had been kept at an ideal temperature and required minimal wing beats to get to their working state. Energy was being conserved for their flight.

Each one seemed like a mini skydiver plummeting from the craft at one thousand metres above the ground. It would take a few hundred metres before they could gain control, reduce speed and start to act like their intended natural cousins.

The hatch door was closed quickly. Oliver said, "All released, hatch closed, let's go".

The Coccinelle was now gently powering away. Too much power would draw attention to any observers on the ground with a change in noise and heat signature. The biological fuel mix was altered to provide a little more power.

*

All ten Moths had dropped from the craft perfectly and had landed and congregated within a few hundred metres of each other. Too close together and they could be all targeted by prey or a mist net. Safety in numbers was good, but all the eggs in one basket could be a disaster.

They were communicating effectively with each other working out the plan for travelling towards the Bio-Insect Oil site. Their flight would take approximately two hours of vigorous flapping. They had sufficient fuel for three weeks of non-flying activity and twelve hours of flying. This would be plenty of reserve in case they were blown off course or needed to land and take off again.

A small explosion occurred as one of the devices slammed into a rock face. There must have been some damage to its internal navigation and hazard evasion system. Each of the other nine Moths then needed to readjust due to a lost signal. A simple change in program in their neural networks; there was no emotion in the process, just a change in communication. Now each moth had only to communicate with eight others and the Coccinelle.

"We're one down", said Oliver with a little grown. That's not good after only thirty minutes flying.

He had been monitoring the Moths' progress carefully. He wouldn't be able to do anything if there was a problem other than cause their self-destruction. He hoped that the self-destruct mechanisms had worked on the moth that had lost communication. It would be bad if one was found and suspicions raised. The explosion would render the moth unusable and its purpose unprovable. As time went by he was reassured by the continued transmissions from the forest.

*

Nine Moths to complete the task, nine small brains gathering information and nine devastatingly powerful chemical detectors.

The small swarm, sometimes called a whisper of Moths, progressed quietly. There were no predators about. The Bats may have moved out due to lack of flying prey in the area. What devastation had been caused on this ecosystem already was not known.

The Bio-Insect Oil site was not far away, and the Moths spread out. They wouldn't draw attention to anyone as it was dark, and it was very common for insects to be seen flying towards the site. No eyelids would be batted in their direction easily.

The Moths had been programmed to land on a tree trunk of suitable camouflage. They would need to be high enough up in the tree to avoid being seen readily by any passing entomologist. Entomologists couldn't climb trees easily and grab Moths. Martina did though on her mission, but she wasn't a typical entomologist. There may be other predators though in the forest that would like to find a tasty meal.

It was an important life skill for an insect to land properly. It had taken much work in the laboratory to get the right mechanisms to work to land on a vertical face, especially one with rough bark. Nature had solved that problem many times over.

One by one the Moths landed on a suitable tree. Only one didn't manage the process properly and promptly fell to the ground. It landed on the ground on top of a rock. The Moths thin metal shell cracked open exposing the delicate mechanisms inside. The self-destruct sequence kicked in and the creature exploded. A further part of the team destroyed. Now eight little machines were left.

*

One of the guards had been sitting outside the main site keeping vigilant. Ever since Bear and Martina had been found near the site the security had been stepped up a little. The disgruntled guard had been one of them who had complained about the number of insets at night time, the number of infuriating mosquitos, flappy Moths and other annoying creatures. It was his job now to be outside and he had no choice, but just to pass the time.

His eye was drawn to an orange flash some distance away in the forest. He had been losing concentration, his mind wondering to nicer things. Thinking of comfortable sofa inside with a can of beer in hand watching some movie or other. It wouldn't be long before the shift changed, and he could enjoy himself a little. That is if he could enjoy being in this desolate and dull place. He wouldn't ever be an entomologist and be interested in the outside world.

Had he seen something he pondered? He wasn't sure. It was a dull place and any distraction would be worth investigation.

There had been lots of glowing lights in the forest when he had first come to work there, many little lights glowing, some on the ground and some in the air. Recently though the numbers had dwindled and so seeing a light at night was now more unusual.

He had no clue that an orange glowing light, even only a brief one, would not be a natural light. He had only thought that the lights at night were either on or off and no consideration of its colour.

He dismissed the light. Tomorrow he might have a look in that area where he thought the light had come from. He was more interested in getting his beer if he was honest. He was bored.

Now there were eight Moths left, eight cunning spies secured to trees sniffing the air. A small dispersed team gathering data.

*

The Moths were reasonably large, and each folded their wings carefully back in place over their bodies. The wings had many functions, primarily for flying, but also to keep their bodies warm and to act as camouflage. It was an incredible skill for an insect to identify the correct place to land by sight and feel through their feet. Each insect landed and immediately gripped the bark. Bark had a rough texture suitable for their tiny clawed feet to hook onto. They brought their bodies close into the bark once in a settled position to heighten the camouflage.

Their wings were tucked tight up against their bodies and blended delicately with the bark. Many Moths were brightly coloured to frighten away predators, but these were disguised to blend into the background. The colouration and patterning mimicked the crevasses, shadowing and contouring of the bark very well. It would take much searching to find these creatures. Their position might only be given away with the twitching antennae. They looked like some lichen protruding from the tree.

*

The Moths had all settled in place, all eight of them. They no longer needed to communicate with each other unless something was to go wrong. It reduced energy consumption and would arise less suspicion if any device happened to be listening for radio transmissions. Tonight, there was no listening.

The Moths were all now in detecting mode, although more precisely in chemical sensing mode. They were positioning on the trees to face the large machinery on the hill side in direct line with the funnels. They had the best chance of detecting chemicals floating in the air.

At midnight, the first chemicals were detected. The first pheromones were activating tiny molecular systems in the Moths' antennae. They were chemically analysed and logged. The technology involved with the detection was remarkable and inspired.

Each moth would store information for a few hours. They would log when each signal was detected, its intensity and direction. The data would be compressed, encrypted and a burst of information sent by radio waves in a very directional way to Insect Code's receivers. The Coccinelle was flying high above the sight well out of the way of prying eyes and ears. The Moths sent their signals directly upwards. The minimal signal sent in a dispersed way would be beneficial and less likely to be detected.

The small and silent whisperers worked their detection constantly for analysis later.

THE ENTOMOLOGIST MAKES A FIND

*Who's studying who – peering through a hand lens
you can often wonder who is studying who!*

Bill took a stroll away from the site. He had a strong pull to be an entomologist and to keep finding insects to study in the field. The laboratory work was interesting, fruitful and what got him paid, but his heart lay in using his observation skills.

He had been out at night many times and could recall many adventures and exciting times finding Moths and other creatures. Night time brought out a hidden world not usually seen. It was a semi-hidden world that many people knew nothing about. This made being an entomologist exciting and quirky. Quirky was good, good to be different.

He had his moth net with him. It was steel rimmed with a mouth about fifty centimetres wide. The handle was extendable. He could use it close to himself and quickly extend it for greater reach. A versatile piece of equipment that had little evolved in two hundred years. Sometimes technology wasn't the answer to everything.

He had a super bright head torch. A vital part of his tools to search at night time as human eyes were not very tuned to night vision. He would search the ground, on trees and along the tracks as he walked. It gave him peace to be alone in the forest with only nature to surround him. It wasn't a dangerous place, but his interaction with Bear had caused some intrigue. Was Bear a genuine lepidopterist or did he have some secret. Bill couldn't fathom this at all.

Bill searched about, sweeping his net occasionally and potting a few insects. He was familiar with most of the beautiful insects and most he simply let go. A few though he didn't know and would be taking back to the main building for study later. Maybe a new moth to science or maybe a new moth to capture with the machine. The machine was destroying everything he loved about the forest. He was paid handsomely for his work and for him this was the strongest motivator, not destruction of wildlife.

Something had caught his eye up ahead. He could see high up on a tree some insect. It was large, brown and not something he had seen before. It was too high for him to reach with his net and he couldn't climb from the ground. It was a moth, something large and unusual. What was he to do now to collect it and study it? He couldn't readily find a way to get it. He knew by all luck that if he went back to the main site and got a ladder it would have flown away by the time he got back.

This was a part of his work he was used to. You couldn't always find what you wanted in the field and sometimes you just couldn't get to something your wanted to collect either. Sometimes Butterflies flew over cliffs, or beetles scuttled into crevasses. He would have to leave this moth alone. Maybe he would come back this way in the morning.

*

The next morning when he woke he was thinking about that large moth he had seen on the tree. What was it? Why hadn't he seen such a moth previously? He decided he should go out looking for it after breakfast.

*

Just before dawn various Moths were still active. The robot Moths had been programmed to shift position at dawn every day. They were programmed to fly a few trees away and settle again. It would raise less suspicion if they weren't on the same tree night after night and day after day. It was a wise decision from Insect Code to do this. Nature had evolved strategies for camouflage for a reason and moving about was part of this strategy.

*

Bill took the Land Rover out with an extendable ladder in the back. The guards didn't care about his odd behaviours. They'd seen it all before, Bill doing strange activities in the night and the day.

He drove the few minutes to where he had seen the moth in the night. He found the tree readily as he had marked the ground with an arrow made of tied up grass stems. A little Scouting and tracking skill in action.

He couldn't see the moth so decided to climb up the tree using the ladder to get a closer look. He also knew that insects moved position over time, so he searched about the tree. He could find nothing. The moth was very close by and if Bill had got the wit to turn around and search a few other trees he would readily have seen the moth.

He was disappointed, but pragmatic about it. There would be another opportunity tonight. Perhaps he would watch what was coming into the funnels tonight and collect a few insects for his own fascination and study.

It was a lucky escape for Insect Code and this single moth would have given the game away. They were still one step ahead of Bio-Insect Oil, but only just.

MOTH CODE ANALYSIS

Hymenoptera – a vast group of insects including Bees, Wasps and Ants. They can often be very social and have divided tasks within their groups. The sum of the parts being greater than the number of individual parts

The Moths had been transmitting data quietly and carefully with precision and direction. The Coccinelle had been circling above at six thousand metres. It was above visible levels, with no flashing lights, limited heat trace and was not detected.

The data had been logged by Oliver. He had been receiving now only seven data sets on each pass. There must have been a further malfunction on one of the devices. The other seven Moths could not diagnose the problem, so it was likely that there had been a chip error. The fall from the Coccinelle the other night had been a challenge for any mechanical device. He was pleased that seven had survived so long so far.

The Coccinelle had done several circles each night before returning to its base with the collected data. There had been no visible traces of being detected.

At the base the data was quickly downloaded onto the main network for analysis. Seven Moths each receiving detailed data and then processing it was starting to turn into a large data set.

The network though had connected to it several powerful machines. These had included various neural networks to digest the data cleverly in more subjective and less analytical ways.

After each data collection and analysis session there was a briefing session. All the crew, scientists and Oliver, Martina and Bear had joined together to figure out what was going on and what could be done next.

Today was no exception.

"Let's summarise where we are with all this then", the head started off in his usual casual manner. He seemed relaxed, but underneath his mind was racing with all the collated information, he could feel they were getting closer now to some action.

"We know Bio-Insect Oil's intentions. We've had that clear all along. They've extracted a huge amount of insect life from this forest and we're already starting to see some changes. The Moths we've planted in the forest have detected fewer and fewer natural pheromones from the native creatures and we continues to pick up the same strength of signals from the machine."

"The Moths have been invaluable for evidence gathering. They've told us the pattern of times when the machine is working. It's been so predictable that they've left themselves open to attach easily."

"The machine starts sending out its pheromones every six hours and on the hour. Local time this is midnight, six in the morning, mid-day, six in the evening and then again at midnight. Each cycle starts with the pheromones being blown out into the forest to the initiation of the mini-migration of the insects. It takes about thirty minutes and then they turn off the fans. For the next four hours, they then start collecting the insects. The fans are reversed to suck them in."

"It's just so awful," said Martina. "It just grates with everything we do to help our planet".

Bear added, "Definitely. It's just so sad. This Tycoon's going to have to pay for all the damage he's done."

"Bear's work with the Butterfly study was superb. It worked a treat and we got all the information about the site we needed. Martina's work on the Grasshopper too was superb getting all the timings right for the workers. The Dragonfly has been in place for some whilst disrupting the signals. It seems the Tycoon has been focused elsewhere and hasn't thought to investigate why some of the data coming back hasn't been getting through uncorrupted. It's too far for him to go out there to see and to be honest he doesn't seem like a forest dweller to me."

"Yeah, more like pond life", laughed Oliver.

"Hey, don't be rude to pond life", snapped Martina. "You're sinking to his level with a lack of intelligence."

"I know, I know. Just trying to lighten the air a bit." Smirked Oliver.

"So, what now then?" the head asked.

"We've got loads of evidence haven't we that the crazy machine is destroying the environment?" said Bear.

The head looked towards the scientists.

"We think so", they replied. "We've a mass of data, enough to robustly answer your question."

"We should have a vote on this then. So, who thinks we should take further action?"

Bear and Martina had been in the field and seen for themselves the evidence and quickly raised their hands. Oliver wasn't far behind. He'd processed a load of data and figured that something had to be done. The scientists already had their hands up smiling.

"So, I'll raise my hand too", the head said as she lifted his into the air. That's decided then we're going to do something about this now."

"We've got this new device", he continued, "to show you. It's very extraordinary. We think you'll be impressed and I think it's time to bring this out now for you all to see."

One of the scientists went out the room and fetched a box. It was a plain box and a label on the outside was clearly visible. It said, 'Live Robots – beware poisonous'.

"This sounds very ominous", said Oliver.

"This box contains our latest development", said the scientist.

"It's a type of Hymenoptera", he continued, "a type of Bee if you will. But it is no ordinary Bee. We've manufactured this as a robot that can fly like a Bee, look like a Bee and definitely sting somewhat like a Bee. It's got our artificial intelligence in it."

He opened the box and lifted out a transparent box inside of which lay a still Bee-like insect. Its body was segmented and striped black and yellow. He then pulled out a small tablet computer and turned it on. The screen flashed up with a simulated Bee. He tapped the power button for the Bee and it started to warm up by flapping its wings.

He opened the lid of the box and the three, Oliver, Martina and Bear, all instinctively took a step back. The Bee was buzzing loudly wanting to get out of the box.

The scientist then tapped a few buttons explaining that the Bee would now fly about the room and find the flowers. He pointed to the energy level in the Bee, which was at half full capacity.

The Bee buzzed up and started a search pattern around the

room. It was a simple room with a table in the middle, a jug of water, some fruit and some flowers. It didn't take long for the little insect to find the flowers and it landed on one of the flower heads. It then buried itself down the flower trumpet. They couldn't see what was going on, but the energy indicator on the tablet slowly rose a little. The Bee then came out of the flower and buzzed over to another one. Again, the energy indicator rose a little more. This it repeated for all the flowers, six in all. It then moved out into the open space again. The Bee had remembered which flowers it had visited and did not waste time revisiting a flower. A complex memory was required for this to happen, many thousands of interconnected neurons firing in a synchronised way.

The Bee then searched the room and the display indicated that the Bee was struggling to find more energy sources. The scientist then opened a screen showing some sort of targeting device on the Bee. He programmed it to search and find an orange that was in the fruit bowl.

The Bee buzzed up again, searched and readily found the orange this time. What the Bee could see was displayed on the computer screen. The Bee circled the object making some calculations and surveying the scene.

The Bee's behaviour then changed dramatically. It turned into an aggressive creature, its sting pointed downwards and was extended outwards a little. The wings beats changed, and the noise increased as it hovered.

Then it injected its sting directly into the orange. The Bee then flew back to the transparent box.

The orange fizzed a little.

The scientist said, "That was a simple injection of alkaline, something like milk to neutralise the acids in the orange."

"I think I'm getting the idea now", said Bear. "You'll release these insects to go and inject some sort of liquid poison onto the funnel machine to stop it from working."

"Yes, that's spot on", said the head. "It's this, but so much more. You see these are self-sustaining Bees, you saw it take nectar over there on the flower. The Bee can recharge itself from many different sources. This is not a stand-alone Bee though, it works with its colleagues, its friends and the rest of the swarm. These are truly social robots. It can connect to up to three thousand Bees at one times in a perfect biological system. We can pro-gramme these guys to find a specific item at precise place and then inject something to do a job. We can send acids, enzymes, in fact anything you can think of that can be carried and in-jected."

"That's amazingly cool", said Martina. "What have you in mind for the sting to destroy the funnel?"

"We have a simple idea", said one of the scientists. "We've got a cocktail of chemicals able to dissolve certain metals, namely copper used in wiring as well as plastics. We think targeting the wiring of the machine will destroy its capabilities. They'll not be able to remove the melted cables from the floor, something like chewing gum on concrete. It'll take a long time to get a re-pair out there making the whole venture unsustainable."

"Perhaps you could target the satellite cables too?" Martina sug-gested.

"Good idea. We'd only thought about the machine, but you are right let's hit their communication systems also."

The scene was set now, and the plan formulated. Time would tell if these clever little robots could do the job they had been built to do.

GUARDS!

Team – a group of individuals with their own skills when working together form a stronger power than working on their own. The team is reliant on cohesion. Ants!

The four men were playing football outside the building. They had a small open area which was just about big enough for a game of two against two. There were no goalies, just a couple of make shift goals and a well-worn ball.

Bill was a poor player and the three guards mediocre. Their bravado though meant they thought they were good. In fact, they thought they were good at a lot of things, but in reality, were useless. Not even good at being guards and by all accounts that was the simplest part of the whole operation.

Bill was often distracted when playing outside with the others and often lost the ability to be part of a team. There were only four of them, so he was needed to make up the numbers. He would often see a bug flying past or creepy crawly wandering past and scoop it up. His Butterfly net was always at hand and a pot or two in his pocket to retrieve things for examination.

It infuriated the others that he kept doing this. They were simple folk and just wanted to play football. They weren't interested in any of this entomologist stuff, whatever that was. Bill had tried to explain pheromones, antennae and many other things to them, but they didn't get it. He just gave up trying.

They had their job to do and he had his. That's the way it had to be.

"Hey Bill! Come on now come back to us. We're playing as a team remember." One of the guards was getting frustrated.

"Just a minute", he casually said. Bill was on his hands and knees again.

One of the other guards called, "next time you're in the dirt, you're really to have a good look at it. Real close." He laughed heartily. "Come on Bill, just a few more goals and we'll be done."

"Yeah in a minute", Bill wasn't paying much attention. He had seen a lovely Millipede with its legs all synchronised to propel it along. The legs all moved in a ripple effect. It was an efficient and graceful way to travel. It always captivated Bill how these all worked. How was it wired up and programmed?

"Thud!". The ball hit him in his side and Bill called out falling flat on his face into the dirt.

"I told you you'd be studying that closely didn't I", the guard laughed out loud again.

The guards walked off disgruntled. Bill was wiping the mud from off his face and he was checking for bleeding.

"Idiots", he muttered to himself. "They've no idea what's here, just interested in beer and the ball. Why couldn't we have got intelligent thugs instead of these bullies?".

No one heard him. It was just him and this jungle in front of him. A jungle with fewer and fewer insects about. He was lucky to find this Millipede to keep his interest going. He'd not seen a live Butterfly for some while now. It was getting disheartening. He'd signed up for this though and was getting paid handsomely for his expertise.

He was bored and on the verge of anger now. What could he do to get his own back on these brutes. They'd always beaten him at football and always insisted he played although he had never wanted to.

Some wag had sent a box of supplies a few days ago with some jokey things. It wasn't even April fool's day. Maybe one of the guards had ordered something on line so he could play pranks on the others.

'Who knows what goes through their minds', he thought himself. 'If anything at all.'

He had seen in the box and had dismissed everything as childish and nonsense. He now brought back some memories of what he saw and decided it was his time to play some tricks. He knew someone had ordered a dozen rubberised bugs. Toys you get in museum shops to remind you of the visit there. Usually dinosaurs, grasshoppers or squishy bugs. All of them cheap and suitable as pocket money mementoes.

He decided to string them all up about the guards bedroom when they were all asleep. He knew they would be dosed up on their revolting fizzy beer and that they slept soundly. Not soundlessly as the beer made them snore and snore loudly and every night.

Bill often went out at night to find bugs and nocturnal creatures. He knew they wouldn't be checking on him in the night-time when not on duty. There should have been a guard on duty at all times, but he knew they enjoyed each other's company too much to be a single and a twosome rather than a threesome.

*

In the early hours his plan worked. He'd been up early as always working on his machine and heard three grown men crying like babies. At first one called out. He must have been first up and started to go off to the toilet.

The light flicked on, although day light was coming in through the skylights. All three guards were sleepy and bleary eyed. Their low intelligence and still being in a state of low awareness made for hilarity listening to their lack of understanding.

Bill had strung up all the bugs from the ceiling. He was amazed really that none of them had stirred much when he entered their room. He had night vision goggles on that meant he didn't need to turn on the lights.

"Bill!", shouted one of them. "We've had enough of these stupid critters. You nearly made me wet myself. You'll pay for that." He knew he would. Maybe he could plan something more tonight. Some other little prank.

BEE SWARM

Swarm – A vast coordinated collection of creatures, usually insects, working as a collective to achieve a goal together. Often a swarm is used to move a whole colony from one place to another

Swarm technology had emerged a decade ago and the technology had advanced quickly. Bee swarms had been developed to study the behaviours of flying swarms in three-dimensions rather than the traditional two-dimensional table-top type swarms. The processing power and artificial intelligence in these devices was now very powerful and all self-contained.

A new secret aspect had recently been introduced and had extended the usefulness of these swarms no end. They could now refuel on the wing and were fuelled by nectar, just in the same way a natural Bee could do so. These Bees could hover in front of flowers of many different types and sup the nectar. It had been a challenge to ensure they could obtain their nectar from as many different types of flower as possible. There were open flowers, closed flowers, flowers with bell shapes and those with long tube-like structures and the nectar was deep down. The bright idea was to use a telescopic proboscis to get the nectar.

Flowers had evolved to attract the insects to take their pollen away for pollination and their reward was the nectar. If the nectar pool is deep in the flower, then there would be the greater possibility that the pollen would be taken up at the same time rubbing on their bodies and legs. Some incredible evolution had developed little sticky pollen sacks that stuck to Moths' eyes and these Moths were highly specific for certain plants.

The intelligent trick was to make a system to collect the nectar that did not involve the need for a specific insect for a specific plant, but a general feeder that could take advantage of as many plants as possible. The scientific team had done an extraordinary job at getting this achieved and at a microscopic scale. The telescopic proboscis could reach fifty millimetres in length and tuck itself away neatly and was extremely lightweight.

In flight fuelling for a Bee swarm was brilliant and going to be put to good use today.

*

Three thousand robotic Bees had all been set out ready for flight. The task to get them all initially fuelled had been pain staking. Each one had to be fed with a single drop of liquid honey. The honey was not special in anyway, just pure organic liquid packed with energy. Once initial fuelling had been done they could be autonomous. Each one registered to the super computer and then let loose in the vast greenhouse. The fuel sources were abundant in the green house. Each Bee buzzed about collecting the nectar until full then came back to the "hive" – the home station. On average the fuel would last each Bee two and a half hours and could be fully refuelled in about twenty-five to thirty minutes. This meant every two hours the Bees would need to forage when out in the field. They could travel some ten kilometres per day either in the day light or at night time. The nectar sources at night would be different and they were already adapted for that.

Once fuelled they could be put in a low energy usage state ready for transportation.

*

The Coccinelle craft was set to go again. It had worked extremely well in getting Bear to the target area. This time there would need to be a little more control from a local agent in the craft to get them going. Having a mass of communications from three thousand communicating Bees across the airwaves would cause a few eye brows and suspicions to be raised. Once set they would be autonomous within the swarm. Each Bee would be able to act alone if lost from the swarm, for instance if it had not found enough fuel when foraging together.

The swarm was a more complex collection than initially considered. Different Bees would have a different set of computation to enable different and diverse decisions to be made. A leader Bee would be able to navigation and use its energy for that purpose whilst the Bees under its command would use energy for simple monitoring of their own systems and flight.

The Coccinelle came in low this time over the valley some twenty kilometres from the target site. Low as to minimise the distribution of the Bees to enable as compact a group as possible. In the craft the rear door needed only to be opened about ten millimetres high and would be wide enough to let a rapid stream of Bees out. The controller in the Coccinelle simply sent a local signal and the Bees were all activated from their sleeping state and ready to go. There was no need to warm them up like real Bees as the cabin had been kept at the optimum temperature. The flight in was easy and the Bees dropped in place with ease.

The swarm was about ten metres long when dropped from the craft, with three thousand Bees fully functioning. They were about fifty metres above the ground. Their journey would consist of two days of foraging and flight.

*

The Bees hummed about, gaining control and coordination. Soon they appeared like a Starling murmuration. The murmur from the Bees was apt. Although there were three thousand Bees their noise was relatively quiet. The little squadrons with their leaders moved together swiftly and in a very coordinated way. As the wind changed slightly they could all move in a smooth and controlled curve.

They initially came down to mid-tree height, not so close to the ground that they couldn't manoeuvre easily and not too high that they would be adversely affected by changing wind currents. They would need to navigate around the trees, but generally would find tracks, streams and glades to travel along all with open flight paths. Their in-built navigation gave them the general direction of travel.

The Bees climbed up the hills and glided down the valleys. Getting close to two hours of travel the first Bees indicated to their leaders the need for refuelling. Specialised Bees used their power senses to detect nectar sources close by. New little squadrons peeled off the main swarm in search of nectar. They would not go far from the main route, so they would need to forage close by. As soon as a source was identified they would swoop down and sup as required. If the flower had a suitable landing platform, such as a big open flower or a bell-shaped flower, they would be able to save energy when taking up nectar by resting there. The smaller single flowers would mean they would need to hover and use up lots of energy in the process. Hovering takes up so much more energy than straight flight. The Bees knew that.

Soon the Bees were finished and satiated. They then re-joined the main swarm.

Since it was still night time there were several flying predators about; mostly Bats. Spiders would also take flying insects with their deadly and efficient silk traps. A few Bees were caught in sticky webs and one of their fail-safe abilities was to ooze a corrosive liquid. This would destroy any evidence after a few hours that there had ever been was a robotic Bee about.

The Bats would investigate the Bees. They would send high pitched, high frequency pulses of sound from their larynx and receive the sounds through their extremely evolved tragus. They had not encountered anything like these Bees before and could not identify if these buzzy insects were food. They dived at the Bees, came close in for more detail, but fortunately none were taken. A wise move by the Bats as the corrosive chemicals would corrode their stomachs.

The night time slowly changed through a glowing dawn into a full day time. The flora now changed and became richer in nectar. There were few specialised flowers in the daytime and re-fuelling became more straight forwards.

The losses were low in number and a few had succumbed to various random malfunctions. A little wastage was inevitable. After the first day, nearly two thousand nine hundred and fifty Bees remained and fifty corroding bodies lay in the forest. They wouldn't be found.

It would not be long before their target would be in full view.

DRAGONFLY

Dragonfly – A four-winged insect, a large predator and fast agile flier with multifaceted eyes for accurately finding prey

Long, sleek and slender. The insect clattered its wings on take-off. Pulling through the air it accelerated fast. The broad forewings providing great power and the smaller hind wings providing increased control. The Dragonfly was a master of the air.

In the classroom, the Dragonfly was let loose. It had been programmed to search for a specific man-made object. It could search an area quickly and efficiently. Although a lot of insects had ultra-violet detecting vision, this Dragonfly had a range of vision from infra-red through visible to the ultra-violet to help it detect its target.

Up it climbed, rapidly and steeply. It took a wide sweeping pattern surveying the benches, smart screen and the people. Martina, Bear and Oliver watched closely, whilst the teacher monitored the computer screen. Projected up onto the main screen were several images. There were two main pictures a left and a right eyed view directly from the Dragonfly. Overlaid onto the images were some red and some blue hued moving shapes. These were the representations of the Infra-red and Ultra-violet images. The red glowed from the people and the blue from the various lights in the room. There was not much blue as light technology now shone out a restricted spectrum of light in the visual range only.

As the Dragonfly continued to move about the space of the class-room its wings buzzed a little. On some of the tight turns the trailing edge of the forewing and leading edge of the hind wing glanced past each other causing them to make a small clatter. This was a feature of real life Dragonflies too and a symptom of the rapid turns required for manoeuvring. No damage would be done as the wings were resilient.

As the Dragonfly flew to the furthest point in the room the teacher placed a mini satellite dish on the work bench. The Dragonfly flipped and flew back towards the teacher. Immediately a greenish hue appeared on the main screen around the satellite dish.

The students looked puzzled trying to work this aspect out. The infra-red and ultra-violet colours were obvious, but green hue wasn't.

The Dragonfly quickly aimed for the satellite dish. It made one loop around the dish and then proceeded to land on the top of it.

On the screen, another image popped up. It showed some sort of signal. Presumably this came from the satellite dish.

The teacher tapped a few buttons on his screen. The displayed signal then changed and became scrambled.

"So, class you've seen the power of this new insect we've developed. Insect Code have worked hard on this one. I guess you've worked this one out already. Oliver what do you think".

Oliver dived in, "Well it's a Dragonfly..."

"Yeah really!" interjected Martina. It was her time to get back at Oliver for his jibes.

"Yeah a Dragonfly. It must have Infra-Red and Ultra-Violet sensors as well as visual spectrum. It honed in on that satellite dish. But the dish wasn't on, was it?" He was still puzzled.

"That's right. The Dragonfly used a few different clues here to detect the satellite dish. Using the visible light, it could detect a shape that it recognised, and the IR could help it understand if the sun had been heating it up as would the sun onto any metal object compared to the surroundings. The clever bit though was the ability to detect that radio signals had been used sent in the past twenty-four hours. There would always be some residual signal pattern in the molecules of the satellite."

There had been a lot of research recently about this newly detected phenomenon. Satellite dishes were not hidden devices any more. Send a signal and there would be trace of that signal remaining in the metalwork for some time. New dishes needed to be created to detect signals from a satellite and then not have a memory for that signal.

Bear remembered the motto again: "Make no trace; leave no trace and blend in", but instead this was "Make a trace, leave no trace and blend in". It would be difficult to outsmart this Dragonfly.

"We've set this one up to show you the images and they were transmitted to my computer here and relayed up to the screen. In the field the transmission part would give away the presence of the Dragonfly. In the field insects the transmissions are obviously kept to a minimum."

"OK we've got that now", said Martina, "but what's the point in the Dragonfly finding a satellite dish?"

Oliver became excited now. "Hey, perhaps it's got a disrupting chip. You know one that can interrupt a signal and subtly change it so that a message doesn't get through properly."

"Pretty much that's it", said the teacher. "The Dragonfly takes the signal coming up the wires to the dish and changes them slightly, adds in a few extra signals to make the signal useless or unreadable. Just the same when signals are received: alter them a little and they'll not work."

"That's pretty cool. Liking the idea of a Dragonfly doing this. It can get there fast, be anonymous and sabotage the signal without anyone realising where the problem is coming from."

Bear had a thought. "What do we do if the satellite dishes at the enemy place aren't detectable?"

"We're going to have to take our chances on that one. We've tested this system with many different types and they've all worked. The security systems seem to be in the computer's firewalls and not at the main door!"

"That makes some sense", replied Bear, "the doorways are always the weakest points, the places where things have to go in and out. This is a neat idea."

The teacher powered down the Dragonfly and lifted it carefully from the dish in the classroom. It was stowed away for the technicians to modify further if needed.

DRAGONFLY RELEASE

*Captivity – when insects are caught they will continue
their natural behaviours, trying to get away and this can
cause damage readily. Insects must be looked after carefully.
On release their nature behaviours are set free too*

The Dragonfly was a strong flier but could only fly for a day or so without recharging batteries. It would need to be dropped as close as possible to the Bio-Insect Oil site to minimise flying. It had an important job to do and its power was needed for all the disruption it would be making later.

The Coccinelle had been used a lot for the surveillance work and tonight's fly past would have one more passenger. It was small, could rest comfortably on a person's hand, but weighed quite a lot. The Dragonfly was nimble, but the power needed for all the equipment meant for a heavier than expected device.

The Dragonfly was dropped from the craft and it plummeted earth wards. It didn't tumble though, and its flight was controlled for a fast descent. At one thousand feet above the ground it deployed several strategies to slow down.

Firstly, a small parachute opened. This reduced the rate of descent to a third, still not enough for sensible flight. Reports had been obtained of a sixty kilometre per hour Dragonfly in nature. This though was unconfirmed. A controlled and efficient flight would be more like ten kilometres per hour.

The Dragonfly opened its wings, and this stopped the twisting rotating movement in the air. It could gently come up into a soaring flight path. This in turn reduced the flight speed. Once the speed came down to below thirty kilometres per hour the parachute was released. It would not be found in the vastness of the forest and even if it was found no one would know what it was used for. It was against the grain of Insect Code to leave some waste in the forest, but this was a one off and the trade-off was the final mission objective.

The Dragonfly obtained control of its flight and it orientated itself readily. Its objective was not too far away, maybe thirty minutes' flight time at low level.

Its flight would be challenging due to all the trees and the darkness. Fortunately, tonight it was cloudless, and the moon and stars shone brightly. Despite the brightness, the insect robot could navigate in any level of light with its low light sensing abilities.

It twisted and turned readily in the night sky avoiding the trees and undergrowth. It had a small-scale radar at his nose almost turning it into a bat like creature. Its electronics were fast and needed to be to avoid obstacles at a speed of twenty kilometres per hour.

It wasn't long before it arrived at the site. The Dragonfly had been programmed to get to its target quietly and stealthily. What it was not able to do though was avoid the random movements of people.

One of the guards had been sitting out dreaming away at the stars. There had been a few meteors streaking through the sky and this was enough to keep his mind occupied.

The guard was more settled in the forest now with fewer bugs about, fewer little annoying buzzing beasties in his ears. He was no longer scared to be about outside at night time.

He had a can of beer in his hand and had been sipping for some while. Judging by the small pile of finished cans beside him he had been sipping for some while and alone.

Despite his slightly intoxicated state, his mind was drawn to a noise to one side. It was the noise of an insect, this in itself wasn't unusual, but the noise reminded him of those large predatory Dragonflies he kept seeing in the day time, especially near the pond area. The wings clattered in the characteristic way.

He pondered why a Dragonfly would be flying about at night. He had never seen or heard one at night. Maybe he hadn't thought that they would be out when it was dark. He wasn't an entomologist after all.

The creature came in around the side of the building away from the main entrances. It had to fly up and over onto the roof to find its specific target.

The guard shot up from his chair. He now thought that something was amiss. This insect world was a strange one and full of unexpected scary creatures. Scary to the uneducated eye, which his were.

He nearly fell over as his head tracked the insect. The beer had a greater effect than he thought. He remained upright although a little dizzy. He followed the insect as it come close to him.

"It must be a Dragonflea, Dragonfoe! What was it called...yes a Dragonfly?" He thought out loud. He couldn't communicate effectively, and no one was listening.

The insect robot flew up and out of sight.

One of the other guards came out to find the first guard performing a little dance.

"I think you've had enough now", he said and grabbed him by

the elbow. "Time to come in now before you get spooked again by the ghosties".

*

It had been a lucky call for Insect Code that the guard was not sober enough to remember any of his little adventure. The Dragonfly settled cleanly on the satellite dish. The dish had been disguised for visible sight, but not from the signals it produced or the fact that it was metallic.

It didn't take long to hack into the signal and then the Dragonfly could start its business.

*

The other guards had been watching a streamed movie in the recreation room. The signal kept dropping, but they had been used to that. The satellite down link was often interrupted as the satellite went out of direct link with the receiver and the machine's data transmissions were of greater importance.

A few dropped frames in a film was nothing of importance. This is what Insect Code had relied upon, a poor data signal and something not unexpected.

The Dragonfly could then inject its deadly weapon of a few disruptive ones and zeroes. This was all that was required to stop an upload of data to the main data centre. It was a subtle trick and would that could not be readily traced. All the anti-virus software was fully up to date, but this was not a virus, but a predator. The site was slowly being sabotaged so that messages would not be getting through effectively.

BEE ATTACK

Sting – a form of poison used by an insect, such as a Bee, to defend itself when distressed or to defend a colony from attack. Bees often having a single use sting and wasps a multi-use sting

Oliver was ready for the next stage in the deployment. His role was to coordinate the insects out in the field and to problem solve if required. There was a significant amount of autonomy in the field already, but sometimes human intervention was required.

The Bee Swarm would attack the base but would not be able to do so until the suction machine was active. The Moths had been set detecting the pheromones from the machine. All the details of the site were collected by the Butterfly and the Grasshopper had detailed the movements of the people. The Dragonfly would be disrupting the signal from the base. There would be minimal collateral damage. The people were not the objective of this important mission, but the mechanics of the oil production from the machine.

*

The Moths were in place. They'd been receiving the pheromone signals for the past week and had started to formulate a plan to when the signals were being received. The Moths had a capability to send out data, encrypted amongst the Grasshopper sounds. They were sent at a random time in the day to reduce the perception of a pattern. A pattern would be tracked if the signals were sent at the same time every day. Only a small signal was needed. It was stealthy, but also blazon. A signal being sent amongst the enemy arena undetected was unheard of.

*

The Dragonfly had held back. It was some distance from the base. There was now a mental map stored in its circuitry of where all the satellite dishes were on the base. It seems like there was one that had been used for most of the external communications. It could fly there in less than ten minutes. It would never be seen or detected.

*

The Bee swarm had held back too. There was still a big swarm, now numbering around two thousand eight hundred. There had been a few losses, but not a vast amount. The glades amongst the forest had produced enough nectar for their energy needs. There were very few flying insects near the base as a lot had been sucked into the deadly machine. Fewer flying insects meant fewer nectar feeding insects so there was a lot of nectar still about for the Bees.

Two thousand eight hundred Bees was a lot to feed, but this was a big forest and it had ample flowering plants all blooming at this time of the year. The air in the evenings had been thick with scent from the flowering plants. It was a complex cocktail of different perfumes evolved to attract the different insects.

Noticeably there were fewer predators, fewer Bats, fewer birds and fewer small mammals. The machine had been sucking the life from the forest for many months. Bio-Insect Oil had assumed insects would simply move in and fill up the space from where the old ones had been removed.

One major flaw in their project was that the insects take time to expand in range. Sometimes it takes a year for a generation and may only move a few metres at a time to expand their territory. Sometimes the natural balance was upset with more predators or fewer flowering plants of importance to a particular creature. There was an ebb and flow about the balance. The assumption of a replenishing forest was all about flow but had not been as rapid as had been predicted.

*

Oliver sat ready at his console on board the Coccinelle. He had an array of monitors. This was the data centre and control centre. There would be little information received once the mission was in full flood. It would not need human intervention unless something went wrong. Maybe it was going to be easy for him, just sit back with his refillable water bottle. Soda was banned now; environmentally disastrous with one use plastic cups, plastic straws, fizzy water releasing carbon dioxide into the atmosphere and all those sugars. The world had moved on in some ways, but destruction of the environment still continued in other ways.

Oliver had been one of those people in the past with a soda cup at hand always sipping away. The world was now a changed place and much more educated in the ways of health. Twenty-years ago, there would have been an unfit, over-weight man here, but modern times meant modern attitudes to health. Lean and fit of body meant agile of mind.

The first monitor had the site map, an aerial view of the base. Clearly could be seen the camouflaged base with the detail entered as per the information from the Butterfly mission. It was clear now from the satellite shots where the weapon was located and the data from the Dragonfly showed the communications aspects with the satellite dishes. The Grasshopper information had also been helpful showing the human movements. The map was animated with the estimated movements. The times when the patrols returned; the times when the insect goo was taken away and various other movements around and about the building. Insect Code hoped that this information was good and repeatable from day to day. They had trusted the information gathered and their predictions would be tested today.

The animations, it was thought, would be critical to the timing of the attack by the Bee swarm. Get it right and there would be no people hurt, get it wrong and...well who knew what would happen. The Bees carried their little loads full of corrosive material and would cause significant harm to any humans in contact with the chemical.

Oliver would need to be on hand to give the master signal, the one to start the attack. He felt like a General, but then reminded himself this wasn't a military war, but a war on environmental destruction. A war that was sapping this forest and who knew how many other forests too at the same time.

*

Martina was listening to her music again. Her head phones had been firmly secured to her head when the call came in. She had been listening to her upbeat music that motivated her on a daily basis. She voiced a command and was able to speak in a hands-free mode with the head of Insect Code.

"Good morning ma'am", she said politely. "What can I do for you?"

"We are good to go. We just need the voice command from you to initiate the lock down sequence."

It was a new security measure in the systems that four voices had to be heard with their specified messages. Also, they had to respond to a random couple of questions. It would be easy to record someone's voice digitally and play it back to bypass a voice recognition system. Add a Turing test into the system by asking a cleverly thought out question, then the response could not be played back from a recording. It would have to be thought about quickly and spoken with natural tone.

The system worked. Her voice had got through the security system and now the head repeated with Oliver and with Bear as well as himself.

The four voice codes now unlocked the security setup for the Bee swarm. A signal was sent to the Coccinelle, again flying high above the forest. Oliver received the signal and various red markers on his screens changed to green. He was all set to go, all he had to do was make the final decision, was everything in place, was everything working, was there anything not right to stop the mission.

He scanned his screens, double checking everything. There were no issues, nothing to stop him from progressing.

There was a 'Mission Proceed' button on one screen and he pressed this. Extra security was now in place and the system needed a retina scan and thumb print recognition. These were everyday security items, quick, efficient and secure.

The control systems send out a burst of information to the Bee swarm, which reacted instantly. Most of the Bees had a good amount of energy left in their reserves and they fired their wings into action.

Ten minutes and they would be at the site.

The noise of the swarm was getting more intense. More than a buzz now and more of a drone.

The guards were used to strange noises from the forest. They had got used them all over the recent months. Their ears had become tuned into the various noises and anything unusual may mean a sign of trouble. Perhaps an engine of a car or the jets from an overhead plane. Bill had ensured their senses were heightened with regular checks and tests now following the two previous major lapses in security.

The Dragonfly had also been activated. It had been pulled away from the site the evening before. This would minimise the chances of discovery at a late stage in the mission.

The Moths had all been instructed to fly away from the site and locate themselves at rendezvous tree some three kilometres away. If the mission was successful, then they would be collected later. If all things went wrong, then they would be turned into self-destruct. Being located together their tree would start to burn and all trace of their existence removed, melted away and burnt into the atmosphere.

The Dragonfly powered its way to the site. It was much faster than the Bees. Now it would be at greater risk in the day light. If it was spotted and caught the mission may well fail.

It flew rapidly and found the satellite dish quickly. It settled there and quickly engaged with the signals. A stop was put to the signals this time and not disrupted. Communication would be cut.

The Bee's drone increased, and the guards became more interested. There were two of them outside now and calling the third.

The timing had been good, the machine wasn't working at this moment and the delivery vehicle had left some while ago. The guards were in a bit of a down time and not being very alert. Bill was in his rest quarters after another night out under the stars. His alarm would go off in a couple of hours, but his sleep would be disturbed shortly.

The third guard wasn't appearing, and the noise was certainly getting louder, much louder than anything they'd heard in the forest so far. They could now see an angry buzzing mass coming their way. Their flight or fight mechanisms weren't kicking in yet and they stayed outside watching the approaching cloud. What was it all? Was it another of Bill's insect tricks? They didn't know.

The Bees were within a hundred metres and they did not seem to be stopping or changing course. The Bees were coming in angrily now directly towards the guards.

The guards' attention was now drawn to running away. They turned their backs on the Bees, which were approaching fast.

"Run", one of them called. "They're after us."

They clattered their way to the open door of the building. The observations from Insect Code had shown that the building was often left open. The least secure way into a place was through the door and this door was wide open.

The Bee swarm divided into three. Two clouds went towards the funnels, the entrance way for the fooled insects that lead directly down into the machine. They were giant fly traps with an intoxicating and delightful scent leading the insects to their death at the end of the funnel.

The third Bee swarm took towards the door. The open door and sloppy security.

The guards had no idea what this was all about. They flailed their arms about trying to get the Bees away. They didn't know that the Bees had no intention of harming people.

A few Bees were swatted and brought to the ground. They fizzed as they hit the ground and a little smoke came from them. One guard took a moment to study a fallen Bee.

"Bee's don't fizz when they are destroyed?" He called out loud. "There's something weird going on here."

He tried to call to the others, but they had gone. He pocketed a Bee for later examination. It was not moving and assumed it to be dead. Whether dead was the right word to describe them or not he didn't care now. He just wanted to run away.

The Bees were all over the main laboratory. There was no time now to run and get help. One of the guards had managed to get to one of the computers and shut the door behind him. He inadvertently trapped a dozen angry Bees in the room with him and he was becoming more scared.

The computer took its time to turn on. Time was going slowly for the guard with his sense of panic. He also had a radio and screamed into it.

"There's a bug in the system," screamed the guard. "We're being over whelmed by Bees in here. Bill where are you? We need your stupid help with these things. There's something wrong out here. These are some sort of mechanical things not real Bees. Bill, where are you?"

"I'm here, wait a second. What's going on? I was asleep. What's all that noise?" He sleepily radioed back.

"Get here now we need you," the guard replied.

"Right, erm two seconds. Need clothes on."

Bill raced out of his quarters to find the laboratory filled with a mass of buzzing and angry sounding Bees.

"Damn," he said. "What are these things?"

As an entomologist, he knew a lot about insects. He'd seen Bee swarms when out looking for insects. They were usually seen when the queen had decided to move from her hive to find a new place for her colony to settle.

This, though, was not normal activity. Were these Bees angry at something? Had one of the guards disturbed a nest somewhere by poking it?

He then remembered the words the guard had screamed through the radio: 'some sort of mechanical things not real Bees.' What had that meant? He had been asleep and couldn't process that information then, he was starting to see clearly now.

A few Bees lay on the floor having been swatted. He had a quick look. Indeed, they were not natural things, quite heavy and the exoskeletons were clearly visible and made from metal!

He ran to his main computer. This was already turned on and the guard was sitting there.

"Get a message out quick, we're under attack". He instructed the guard.

"I am, I am", he tersely replied. "There's a problem with the link. There's no signal."

"What!" Bill cried. "Try again."

"I have, several times. Someone's blocking the signal somewhere."

Bill ran from the room, looking for some answers. All he saw was the start of some devastation. There was a greenish liquid oozing over the laboratory equipment. There were chemical reactions going on. These were definitely not natural Bees, they were bombing the equipment with some acid to destroy the workings.

The Bees that had entered the funnels were causing a similar amount of damage. The machinery at the end of the funnels was slowly melting away. Clearly the machine would not be operable anymore.

One of the guards had taken a closer look at the liquid coming from the Bees. He had swiped a little up with his index finger and smelt it. It was not one of his cleverest ideas. His finger started to burn, and the pain was agonising.

He ran screaming from the room and plunged his hand into a basin of water. This helped a little, but the chemical reacted with the water causing steam to rapidly come off the surface.

He would regret the decision to smell the liquid for a long time.

*

Once each Bee had deposited its toxic substance, it then flew out of the building. The Bees were significantly lighter now and could fly faster and more agilely. The main door was still open and the exit very easy to navigate towards. Glass had always been a problem for insects, but the sensors in these bees had the added advantage of a pre-loaded map of where to go and where not to. They didn't bump into the glass.

The Bees flew out away from the site back to their rendezvous site. Of the three thousand bees that had started their journey and the two thousand eight hundred that had entered Bio-Insect Oil's site, then just over two thousand were still left flying.

Some of the Bees had deposited their lethal cocktail on top of other Bees. Maybe a flaw in their programming or just a significant challenge to maintain awareness of so many busy insects in close proximity.

*

The toxins used took several days to finish digesting any substance they met. Once the chemicals had worked then they became a solid amorphous mass. These would eventually biodegrade safely and without trace. 'Make no trace; leave no trace and blend in'. Future generations would not know that Insect Code had been here.

MISSION DEBRIEF

Debrief – evolution doesn't have a memory of the past, only a set of codes stored in the DNA of life. There is no reflecting on the past, only status of the present. Human's had developed the ability to achieve by learning and failing from things in the past

It had been an amazing success. Insect Code had successfully defeated a rogue Oil Tycoon bent on destruction and deceit. The Tycoon had not found out about the lack of supply of oil until one of the supply vehicles had made a trip to the site. Deliveries could not always be undertaken by the drone and occasionally a land vehicle was required, especially when transporting people. Insect Code knew they could get people in and out of the jungle with their technology, but Bio-Insect Oil needed drones and Land Rovers.

The word then came back quickly about the destruction of the site. The Tycoon was soon arrested after that. His jungle site was hidden for a while. But he was easy to find.

The guards had done some clearing up. The one guard with the damaged finger was starting to recover although his hand was heavily bandaged. Their work was futile as the site was so significantly damaged by the chemicals that a reinstallation would be required.

Bill had been found cowering in the building ashamed of what had happened. He had realised that his work was now worthless, and the project was finished. It would take many years for him to fully recover. He would never work in this field again and never again where insects ruled.

*

The head of Bio-Insect Oil had brought together the members of the team for a debrief at the headquarters. The public knew now that this Tycoon was single minded-idly set on insect destruction to make his Black Gold rather than the Green Gold. This he had kept from the world.

"Some statistics to start with", the head started to tell the team.

"We believe that the site was fully running for one hundred and sixty days before we stopped its production. Some ten barrels a day were produced giving six hundred barrels. That equates to a lot of insects. Let me see that's about how many…"

He was interrupted by Oliver. "Yeah, we know, we get it. Just thank us. That's all we need."

"Of course," said the head. She grinned as she started. "Insect Code is privileged to have found you extremely talented and skilful people. Martina your agility and musical analysis has been second to none. Oliver you've carried your wit with you all the way, yet your technical skills have been profound. Bear you have inspired a great deal of this work. We have a lot to learn from history and history will repeat itself again in the future."

"What more can I say? We did it guys."

"And girls", joked Martina. They all laughed.

What a team they had been.

MEDIA COVERAGE OF BIO-INSECT OIL'S DOWNFALL

Survival – in nature there are winners and losers. Evolution is about finding a dynamic balance. Sometimes big and strong survives, sometimes small and quiet sneaks through and the at other times a little bit of cleverness is all it takes

A spokesperson was now standing up in front of the media. There was a reasonable crowd gathered. This time there would be no rudeness from the presenter and no one would be banished from the room. The previous time Bio-Insect Oil was the centre of attention in the room, the presenter had been the Tycoon heading up the business.

"Hello, my name is Millicent Angelique and I am the spokesperson for Insect Code. You may not have heard of this organisation. We are an organisation that has now successfully neutralised Bio-Insect Oil."

Millicent was a red headed woman with a strong assertive character. She was engaging and immediately captured the audience's attention.

There was a small gasp from the audience. You will remember that the main man of Bio-Insect Oil...", she paused to put up the first photograph on the screen, "...was an Oil Tycoon called Henry Collinsdale and spun to you all that this revolutionary product called Bio-Insect Oil would be the fuel of the future from a sustainable energy source, namely insect pests. We have gathered significant evidence from the field at the site shown here." She brought up the next slide showing the site in its working state.

"This picture was created from various satellite and other covert operations. The details of which we won't go into here today. You can see these large funnels at the front of the building. These have been used to send out chemical messages into the forest to attract a wide range of insect life back into the funnels. The machinery behind the funnels then crushes the insects."

There was an amount of shuffling in the audience as they were becoming a little uneasy about it all now.

She continued, "The crushed insects are then made into the oil known as Bio-Insect Oil. You were all told that the insects would be taken from places where they are pests. We now know that this was economical with the truth and that the insects were simply taken from the forest without care or regard for which insects were taken."

Various hands shot up at this point.

"I promise that I'll take questions in a moment or two. A few more things to cover first."

"Most of the research had been done by the well-respected entomologist, Bill Woodly. You may have heard of him. He's presented on a few television documentary programmes about insects." She brought up a further picture of the man.

"We used our technology and Special Forces to gain entry to the site and detail the site layout." She brought up Bear's Butterfly map showing the site as laid out as the Obtulate Butterfly.

"What you see here is a disguised map of the site. If you can look closely you can see the location of the funnels and doorways for the machine."

The audience was becoming more interested now by this clever use of an old-fashioned spy technique in this modern era.

"We'll tell you some other time how we came across this idea and where it had previously been used. All I can say at this time is to Be Prepared."

"We monitored the site here for a while and realised the destruction that it was causing to the local fauna and decided to take assertive action to disable the machinery. We're not a destructive organisation but have managed to stop production and am now bringing this to your attention."

"So, time for some questions."

She was asked about various aspects of the evidence gathering, some of which she could answer and some which she could not. She was also asked about the Butterfly site map and gave the reply that this Butterfly seen here is a rare Bbeeutterfly and we now know more about it scientifically than previously and that was a bonus to science. An unexpected outcome.

She was also asked about the state of the environment in this forest. She had replied that there had been significant reduction in biodiversity in the site and that the site would be monitored for many years and any remedial action would be taken to restore a suitable ecosystem.

"What is there stopping others from doing the same or something worse next time?" Someone had asked.

"We can only tackle what we know and make it known that Insect Code will be tracking them and monitoring their activities.

We obviously don't want anything like this to happen again, but people's greed will always get in the way of conservation and protection of the environment."

*

It had been a good press conference. The audience had been shocked and then had taken on board the spin from Bio-Insect Oil. A company now never to exist again in the same way. Insect Code's work though would not stop, it would never stop. There would always be people trying to exploit planet earth for their own purpose and not for a balance of nature.

EPILOGUE

Balance – A seesaw is stable, but a little shift in weight can cause the balance to be upset. The balance can be restored with a further shift in weight back. A seesaw may never be stable

The forest had an annual check-up. The site was monitored for its biodiversity quality. A team of experts were sent every year to find out progress with rewilding of the place. There were ornithologists, mammal experts and definitely entomologists each with their own set skills and expertise.

Each person in the team had three days of intensive study to investigate the site, draw up some quantification of the biodiversity and report back.

They would make the same transects that they had done for the past few years starting from ten kilometres out from the old base and walking directly, or as near directly to it as possible. Then taking notes along the way of observations close by ten kilometres was quite tough in these conditions and studying at the same time. Each carried their own back packs of camping equipment for the night shift.

The ornithologist carried high powered binoculars, several guide books and a high-quality camera as well as the Global Positioning Satellite locating device and notebook.

The mammal expert's job was a little different. She had to take note of the tracks on the ground and various feeding signs. She would lay out a small mammal trap every few hundred metres and come back for them the next day.

The entomologist's job was challenging due to the numbers of insects. With his trusty net in hand Bear was efficient and focused on his task. He now enjoyed the entomological work so much he trained hard and was now a full-time expert in the area. No longer did he need the action type of job. This was now much more rewarding.

*

The results took their time to be analysed and conclusions drawn. The first few years indicated a devastation in the insect life. At the full ten kilometres' range, there had been a reduced impact, but close into the base there was significant losses. Many of the Butterflies had been non-existent. It had been a hard time for Bear seeing all the damage made.

The bird populations survived well the first year, but drastically dropped the next year as there were limited food sources available. The signs of the mammals were equally poor.

Over the forthcoming years though the insect life came back into the affected area. The plant growth had been lush as able to grow with fewer insects eating their way through it all. The insects thrived and boomed causing a vast number in years four and five. The birds then fed well and bred further young.

A cycle continued year-on-year, an ebb and flow of the different organisms. At first it was a huge change, but over time the general trend was good and positive. The biodiversity increased and regained footage in the forest. It seemed that the human impact had been smoothed over by the swift action of a few at Insect Code. A grand lesson in conservation for all.

INSPIRATION FOR INSECT CODE

Entomology is a fascinating subject full of observation, detail and excitement around every corner. Insects are incredibly diverse and found in most terrestrial habitats in the world. If you look closely enough, you'll find insects of many varieties around you now.

There are many ways to study insects, some of which the author has used and practised over many years. A light trap is a common way to draw Moths, and other insects, into an airy box. The Moths can then be studied close at hand and released without harm. A moth trap can be used deep in woodland, on sand dunes, at the top of a mountain or in a back garden. All of which the author has done.

Many insects need to be found by searching. Knowing the available habitat, the plants and season is important when looking for and identifying insects. It is not always necessary to identify everything that is seen and basking in the beauty and diversity is thrilling.

As a Scout Leader the author has known about Lord Baden-Powell's inspiration of young, and not so young, people in all things nature and natural. His formative years was with the military and during some campaigns he was sent out to secretly investigate an enemy encampment. He would then draw that base pointing out the important parts for a raid sometime later. The base would then be disguised as a Butterfly. A clever piece of camouflage in itself.

END NOTICE

No insects were harmed in the writing of this book!

Watch out though for the fly on the wall, you'll
never know what's it's thinking!

BACK COVER

A Butterfly flaps it's wings. A Grasshopper chirrups in the meadow. A Beetle flies across the evening sky. The world is full of insects buzzing about. Insects are common, insects are everywhere.

Greed and money take over people's minds in unexpected ways. Technology is used to destroy the environment.

A secret organisation is set up to destroy a new breed of scientist using their detailed knowledge of the world to aid human's needs for energy.

How will the insects fight back? How can a simple sketch be disguised to help the efforts?

In this novel science and entomology clashes in a new evolution of adventure.

---

[1] Skeletoniser – a moth caterpillar that chews through leaves, but not the veins in the leaf causing only the structure of the leaf to be left behind, like a skeleton

Printed in Poland
by Amazon Fulfillment
Poland Sp. z o.o., Wrocław

52379695R00117